Praise for G

"*Ghosts of War: Retribu*   ...,
revenge, and a complex story that will keep surprising you right till
the end—this is sci-fi done right."

—Craig Munro, author of *The Bones of the Past*

"Playtime is indeed over as violence begets violence in this vivid
futuresque setting. Robinson excels at creating an immersive
off-world experience while inducing a laugh at spinning action
tropes inversely."

—Rick Heinz, author of *The Seventh Age: Dawn*

"'Revenge is a dish best served cold.' Paul Robinson's debut novel,
Ghost of War: Retribution, brilliantly spins this old proverb into an
action-packed yarn that leaves readers salivating for more. Robinson
deftly guides the reader, often through humor and heartache, on an
audacious space romp. I say, bring on the next course!"

—Paul Inman, author of *Ageless*

"*Ghosts of War: Retribution* is an adrenaline-fueled adventure, perfect
for fans of fast-paced action sci-fi."

—Robert Batten, author of *Blood Capital*

"Sci-fi action-adventure at its very, very best. Paul Robinson gives
us complex characters facing complex conflict in a futuristic world
that, although dystopian, always carries the ring of truth. There's
revenge, retribution, heroism, and, sprinkled throughout, satisfy-
ing bits of wry humor. A winning combination, and a debut author
worth watching."

—Jason Pomerance, author of *Women Like Us*

"Paul Robinson thrills his readers in the style of James Rollins
and John Grisham, and then brings them to another world in
the style of Robert Heinlein. You should pick up *Ghosts of War:
Retribution*, though be warned: it's hard to put down. ★★★★★"

—Jonathan Maas, author of *Flare*

GHOSTS OF WAR

RETRIBUTION

PAUL ROBINSON

Published by Inkshares, Inc., Oakland, California
www.inkshares.com

Interior design by Kevin G. Summers

ISBN: 9781947848900
eISBN: 9781947848399
LCCN: 2018932818

First edition

Printed in the United States of America

To you.

(Yes, you.)

/RET-RI-BU-TION/
Punishment inflicted on someone
as vengeance for a wrong or criminal act

ONE

"YOU SURE THE cloak's working?"

"I checked it yesterday. It's fine, mate."

"You only finished installing it yesterday."

"Ramses, are we or are we not currently being shot out of the sky?"

"No, Sol, we are not."

"Well, I guess it's bloody working then, ain't it?"

Cole Traske stood in the back of the cockpit listening to his pilot, Solomon Dane, and demolitions man, Ramses Barden, bicker as they always had. He'd never gotten to the bottom of where the bickering started between them. It was already in full swing when he met them, and it had gone on so long that he couldn't be certain they'd even remember.

"Look," Ram started again, turning to face Sol. "All I'm saying is that I know that *you* know that we both remember what happened on Seris III, and that that time, it wasn't working."

This time, Sol didn't reply and his silence said more than any words could.

A voice spoke up from Cole's left. It was Gregor Mishkol, the first new member of Penumbra in ten years and only the sixth member in the squad's twenty-five-year history. He had been busy quietly cleaning his rifle, and Cole had forgotten he was even there.

"Are they always like this, sir?" Gregor asked.

"Unfortunately, they are, kid," Cole said. "But you'll get used to it."

A shudder rolled through the cockpit as Sol brought the ship closer to the surface. It wasn't usually this rough, but then the *Havok* wasn't exactly designed to fly consistently at this altitude. Nothing Cole hadn't sat through countless times before, though. Ahead, the city was just coming into view, the low, setting sun catching on the endless rows of glass and concrete.

Following a short series of beeps, several displays lit up on the central console and information began streaming across them.

"About bloody time," Sol said.

"Ram?" Cole asked, continuing to look out over the city.

"Target is a Modosian male," Ram said, his eyes never leaving the screen. "Political extremist. Recently been associating with some undesirables he probably shouldn't have been."

"Location?" Cole asked.

"Currently enjoying a lovely evening at the Tragg Empirical Casino. I expect that'll change."

"Directive?"

Ram paused. "Housecleaning with a lookie-loo."

Cole thought for a moment and sighed. "Smash and grab it is then."

"Cole, don't," Ram said, turning his eyes away from the monitor. "Now's not the time to ruffle feathers. After Nate, I don't—"

"It's a smash and grab. No arguments. If they want them dead, they can do it themselves, and if command doesn't like it, they shouldn't have put me in charge."

"They almost didn't," Sol chimed in.

"Fine," Ram said, raising his hands in surrender. "But you're doing the paperwork this time."

"I *always* do the paperwork, Ram," Cole said.

"I know, I know. I'm just saying that this time, *specifically*, you're doing it."

From the rear of the cockpit, Gregor cleared his throat. "Um, sir? Not wanting to interrupt, but just so I'm clear on the details, we're taking the target alive?"

"Apparently so, kid," Ram said as he returned his attention to the monitors.

"And that's going against orders?"

Cole turned to face Gregor who looked visibly uncomfortable. "Is that a problem?"

"Um, no? I mean . . . is that normal? I-it doesn't feel normal. Federation Code says that—"

"One thing you'll learn, kid, is that FedCo doesn't always apply to us. We have certain . . . freedoms."

Sol laughed. "Loopholes, you mean."

"Hey, look," Cole said, stifling a smile, "loopholes, freedoms, call it whatever you want. Point is we have final say."

"So, it *is* normal then?" Gregor asked.

"More or less."

Gregor slumped back against the cockpit wall, but Cole could see something was still bothering him.

"What's up, kid?" Cole asked.

"Why are the orders coming in so late, sir?" Gregor said. "I thought there was supposed to be a forty-eight-hour buffer to allow for proper preparation and—"

"There have been some . . . issues of late," Cole said.

"Issues, sir?"

"Leaks," Sol said over his shoulder. "Targets getting tipped off, things of that nature."

To say there had been some issues lately would be putting it mildly. Acquisition rates across the Forty-Second Unification Division had been at an all-time low for months, and enlisted casualty rates were at their highest point since the end of the Fifty-Year War. These weren't details Cole felt like going into, though. The kid looked spooked enough as it was.

"How far out, Sol?" Cole asked.

"Five minutes."

"Well then," Cole said, moving for the door, "let's do this."

Gregor got up and rushed to the door before he was pulled back by Cole.

"Easy," Cole said, placing a reassuring hand on his shoulder. "First time ain't so bad. Just let it come to you, and you'll be fine."

"Yes, sir."

"And can we please cut it with this 'sir' crap?" Cole asked with a sigh. "You're killing me."

"Yes, sir. S-sorry, sir," Gregor said, tripping over his words. "I, uh—"

Gregor proceeded to shuffle hurriedly out of the room, head down.

"Poor kid. You scared him," Ram said with a chuckle.

Cole laughed. "I was trying to be nice."

"He's gonna be a handful, isn't he?" Ram said, already knowing the answer.

"I told Oren we'd be OK with just the three of us," Cole said. "But y'know—"

"Regulations," Ram said.

"Regulations," Cole echoed.

"Fickle bitch, they are," Sol said as he forced his way between the pair and out into the main hold.

"You said it," Cole said as he made his way out of the cockpit after him.

"Hey, remember, Cole," Ram said, "first time ain't so bad. Nate would be proud of you."

"I hope so."

"He would be," Ram said. "Just . . . keep your head on a swivel, OK? After what happened we need to be careful about—"

"I know. I've got this."

It had been six months since the death of Nathan Revik, their former leader. For six months, they'd been on the bench, a command-sanctioned "grieving and evaluation period." Two months ago, Cole had been appointed the new leader of Penumbra. Today was their first day back on the job.

The *Havok* touched down silently on the roof of the casino. Its boarding ramp lowered, and four figures descended, moving into cover. Then, as quickly as it arrived, the ship glided away to a safe altitude. It was nothing but a faint shimmer in the ever-darkening night sky. The casino roof was empty, and it seemed no one was aware of their arrival.

"Told ya."

Ram gave Sol a short, sharp punch in the arm as his only reply.

It took no time at all to locate a maintenance shaft, and with a quick blast from a plasma cutter, they were inside. They moved in silence, Cole on point, Ram bringing up the rear with Gregor just in front of him.

Sol, however, was muttering to himself the whole time, running his hands along the walls, looking for a jack-in point for the casino's security. It took longer than he'd hoped, but he found it. "Sneaky little bastard."

"Got him?" Cole asked.

"Just a sec," Sol said, flicking through the feeds. "Ah, there he is. Private game room off the main floor."

"How many others?"

"About a dozen. Looks like maybe four security."

Cole moved closer to get a better look at the feed. He scanned the faces of those in the room but couldn't make anything out on the grainy feed. For a reason he couldn't explain, Cole started to get an uneasy feeling in the pit of his stomach.

"Cole?" Ram said, trying to get Cole's attention.

Snapping out of his trance, Cole pulled back from the monitor. "Floor plan, Sol?"

"Uh, yeah, here it is." The main floor of the casino flickered onto the screen as a vague three-dimensional rendering.

Cole looked it over. "Sol, I want you to stay here. Monitor the feeds and get ready to cut the power. Ram, I need you on the floor for crowd control. They'll probably panic."

"They usually do," Ram said, moving off down the walkway.

"Gregor, I w—"

"Yes, sir?" Gregor said, interrupting. Cole just looked at him. He got the message.

"I want you up here, on this mezzanine." Cole pointed it out on the map. "Looks like it's undergoing some renovations, so there should be plenty of cover up there."

A quick nod and Gregor was off running down the corridor. Cole watched as he darted around a distant corner and disappeared. He was young, maybe too young, and this was his first time in the field. The higher-ups had assured him that Gregor was the finest young sniper the academy had seen in years, but that didn't stop him from also being the most nervous young sniper Cole had seen in years. He was, however, seventeen years Cole's junior, so he could be forgiven for being just a little jumpy.

"He's eager," Sol said. "I'll give him that."

"We all were at his age."

It took Cole a few minutes to navigate through the vents above the casino's main floor, being careful not to make too much noise and alert those below him. There was enough noise down there that he probably didn't need to be so careful, but it was always better to be safe than sorry. He'd been shot at in a vent before. It wasn't fun. The three jagged scars in his left calf were evidence of that.

"Everyone ready?" Cole asked over the comms.

"Good to go," came Sol's reply. By this time, he'd gutted several control panels back in the maintenance shaft. It turned out that gaining access to the lights proved to be more complicated than he'd planned. "I'll only be able to get you a few seconds of darkness before the backup kicks in."

"It'll have to do," Cole said.

"I'm ready," Gregor whispered. He had a clear view of the entire main floor from his position. Gaming tables covered the majority of the floor, and there were several large statues scattered about. The private game rooms were along the back wall. There were about ten by his estimation, and he had a clear view of all their doors. To his left a large, two-level walkway stretched into the distance, no doubt leading to some kind of balcony or outdoor plaza. Below him to his right was the bar. It extended the length of the wall, and there he saw a familiar face.

"Ram?" Cole pressed, after not getting a reply.

"He's uh," Gregor stammered, "a bit busy."

"Ram," Cole said, not louder, but more urgent.

"All right, all right," Ram said, farewelling his new female companion with a wink. "Keep your pants on."

"You keep *your* pants on," Sol said, chuckling as he watched the scene on the monitor.

"What can I say? I'm a people person," Ram said, moving away from the bar out onto the main floor.

"You good?" Cole said.

Ram leaned against a giant gold statue by the entrance, giving him a clear view of the whole room. "Yeah, I'm good."

"All right then, wait for my mark," Cole said.

Cole had positioned himself at a ceiling grate, which gave him a relatively clear view of the private room beneath him. The lighting was dim, but he could still make out the individuals inside. Sol was right: a dozen players, two with a pair of private security each. One of them was the Modosian they were after. The short horns protruding from the back of his head made him easy to spot. The guards complicated things, but not dreadfully so.

Cole retrieved the small plasma cutter from his belt, and after a few quick bursts, the brackets holding the grate in place were severed. A barely imperceptible scraping was the only sound the grate made as Cole gently pulled it aside, leaving nothing between him and the room below.

It was time.

"On my mark," Cole said, readying himself, still unable to shake the uneasy feeling in the back of his mind.

"Go."

Darkness. Panic.

The lights went out almost immediately. Cole fell from the ceiling, dropped to a knee, and quickly surveyed the situation. The emergency lighting had kicked in, bathing the entire room in a dull red glow. He blocked out the panicked screams from the patrons outside and made his move.

Guarasci began his official term as provost on August 1, 1997. One of the first things he did was to take a group of key faculty to Washington DC for a conference on core curriculum. This seemed to be the practice of each new provost who came to Wagner. Because the AAC conferences were usually about core curriculum, many MDS professors were chosen to go to them. There were seminars to attend during the day and the whole group went out to dinner together each evening. After dinner the men gathered around the bar. Julie Barchitta, Ammini Moorthy and I played gin rummy after dinner and laughed and joked together.

At the beginning of the fall semester, Dr. Guarasci presented a proposal to the COW for a new undergraduate curriculum. The new curriculum, *The Wagner Plan for the Practical Liberal Arts,* emphasized "learning by doing." Guarasci worked hard to obtain enough faculty who would be willing to teach in the new curriculum. The "learning community" concept was the key feature of this curriculum. Learning communities were thematically linked courses that enrolled a common group of students. There were three components of the learning communities—liberal arts courses, experiential learning and reflective writing tutorials.

Each learning community was to be taught by two professors. Marilyn Kiss and I taught a learning community together. The students in our learning community were divided into two groups. One group took my liberal arts course and the other group took Marilyn's liberal arts course. The second component of the learning community was experiential learning. Students were to be placed in non-classroom settings where they could observe and participate in real life activities related to the content of the liberal arts courses. Marilyn and I taught liberal arts courses about children in difficult life situations. We placed our students in schools and family service organizations to work with children from educationally and economically deprived families. Their experiences related to the biographies of disadvantaged children in our liberal arts courses. By linking course topics to fieldwork in experiential learning, students discovered connections, or conflicts, between ideas and real life situations.

The third component of the learning community was a reflective writing tutorial (RFT). This was to be a new course that each faculty member in the new program would teach in addition to his or her liberal arts course. RFTs were courses where students could relate what they learned in their experiential learning component to their reading assignments through class discussions and writing assignments. By analyzing real life experiences through discussion and writing in their RFTs, students could develop critical thinking and writing skills. Marilyn and I developed our RFT together so that our students would get the same content in both RFTs. Marilyn taught the RFT to her group of students and I taught it to mine.

Our RFT began with the reading of *Call to Service* by Robert Coles, which gave the students some preparation for their experiential learning. Then the RFT dealt with different types of writing. The book, *The Road from Coorain* by Jill Conway was assigned to give examples of beautiful descriptive writing and autobiographical writing. The next topic in the RFT was persuasive writing. Students were assigned Martin Luther Kings's book, *Why we can't Wait* and David Halberstam's *The Children,* a moving biography of nine young people who risked their lives in the civil rights movement. They also watched the films *The Road to Freedom* and *Legacy of a Dream* in class. The students' writings and discussions were effusive in response to these readings and films. The last section of the RFT dealt with helping others and different types of service. Students read *The Bean Trees* by Barbara Kingsolver and the saw the film, *City of Joy.* Students were required to write about types of service and helping others and they gave oral presentations on their experiential learning at the end of the course. The discussions in the RFT course were some of the best in all my teaching experience.

The *Wagner Plan for the Practical Liberal Arts* stipulated that students would participate in three learning communities over the course of their college careers, one in the freshman year, one during the intermediate years and one in the senior year in their majors. The *Wagner Plan* was brought to the COW in October 1997 and accepted by the faculty. The first learning communities were taught to the incoming freshman class in the fall of 1998. During the spring of 1998 several writing workshops were held to prepare the faculty to teach the RFT's. Julie Barchitta was appointed Dean of Experiential Learning. She spent the spring and summer of 1998 lining up experiential learning sites for 500 incoming freshmen. In May Dr. Guarasci invited the 32 faculty who would be teaching in the new program to a retreat. We went to Beaver Farm in upstate New York and spent a week together discussing how to implement the learning communities. We went on a retreat at the end of each academic year to evaluate the success of the new program and talk about ways to improve it. Julie Barchitta and I always roomed together on the retreats. At the retreats Julie talked about the experiential learning, which students were involved in, and discussed with the faculty how to make the best use of the different experiences available. Guarasci held regularly scheduled meetings during the academic year for faculty to share their experiences in the program and discuss strategies for teaching it.

In the spring of each year Julie invited all the agencies that were providing experiential learning sites to come to a luncheon at Wagner. She gave the agency representatives certificates of appreciation and selected students were asked to speak about their experiences. One of my students had a charming video of young children in an after—school program where she taught them how to dance. Other students talked of their experiences and how much they enjoyed working with the children. Julie had an excellent rapport with the agencies' personnel in the community. After three years as Dean of Experiential Learning, she was awarded the Skinner Education Award by the New York Urban League at a fancy luncheon at the Hilton Hotel. In her acceptance speech she mentioned how much she had learned from her two mentors, Drs. Nelson and Schuyler. We both were there and were very flattered.

As the Wagner liaison to the NYU Faculty Resource Network, I discussed our new curriculum with other deans at network meetings. The director of the network asked me to give a speech on the *Wagner Plan* at the Faculty Resource Network National Symposium in New Orleans in November 1999. I was on a panel on *General Education: The First Year and the Core Curriculum for the 21st Century.* I led a group discussion after the panel. I received many compliments on my presentation and Dr. Guarasci told our faculty that he heard complimentary comments on my speech. Mike came with me to New Orleans and worked in the motel room while I was at the symposium. We enjoyed the night life in the city and shopping for souvenirs for the grandchildren.

In the spring of 2000, Dr. Guarasci offered me the position of Dean of the College. I had begun to think of retiring so that I could spend more time with the grandchildren. I considered the position that Guarasci offered, but decided to continue as Associate Provost and Dean of Graduate Studies and retire the following year. Mildred Nelson had also expressed interest in retiring about the same time.

In the fall of 2000 I was asked to speak on Louisa Schuyler to the alumni of Bellevue Nursing School. Louisa Schuyler founded the first nursing school in America at Bellevue Hospital in 1873. I was an authority on her achievements as she was one of the two women about whom I wrote biographies in my doctoral dissertation. Alumni of Bellevue Nursing School had donated a million dollars to the new Center for Nursing History and Nursing Research in Albany, New York. There was a large crowd at the meeting and my speech was well received. The director of the new center, Dr. Cathryne Welch, approached me after my speech and asked me to serve on the planning committee for the new center. I agreed to serve on the committee.

When Mildred and I decided to retire we both went to the president to tell him we were leaving. He was devastated as we did much of the essential work of the college. At commencement in May he surprised everyone by asking Mildred and me to come up to the podium with him at the end of the ceremony. He put his arms around both of us and told the audience that we were retiring. He described us as the "left and right arms of Wagner College." He described the contributions we had made to the college and ended by saying, "Their retirements leave a void at Wagner and they will both be missed by faculty and students." We received a standing ovation for several minutes from the faculty, students, administrators, and trustees. The students dedicated the yearbook to us the following year

At the end of May Mike and I went to Italy for a week with Wagner friends. Professor Geoffrey Coward of the education department had arranged a trip for Wagner students to study abroad in England and Italy during the summer. There was extra room on the plane and tour bus, so other Wagner people were invited to join the group. We decided to go for the second half of the trip in Italy. Some of our favorite people in the college were on the trip including Julie and Roy Barchitta, Mildred Nelson and her niece Evelyn, Mary Ann Kosiba, Valerie and Art Kozma, Dorine and Matt Trivelli and some very nice nursing and education students. Mike and I flew to London and met the rest of the group there following their week in England. We

all flew to Bologna together and were met by our bus driver at
the airport. We stayed in a charming little hotel in Bologna and
enjoyed the complimentary breakfast each day with the group.
Each day the bus took us to another fascinating city.

We toured Bologna, Florence, Ravenna, Venice and Ferrara.
Mike and I had never been to these places and we marveled at
their history and beauty. We visited Europe's first university in
Bologna and heard a lecture in the classroom where anatomy
was taught in the early years of the university. We were awed
by the grandeur and beauty of Florence and delighted with the
charm of Venice. I enjoyed Ravenna where I saw Dante's tomb
and then our bus took us to the seaside. One student and I went
swimming while the others sat on the beach. We ate dinner in
Bologne each evening with members of the group and had a
wonderful time discovering new and delightful restaurants.
When we felt we were spending too much we took a break and
ate in the little cafeteria a block from the hotel.

There were two free days on the itinerary, one after the trip to
Venice and one on the last day. We chose to stay in Venice one
extra day and spent the last day in Ferrara. Mildred and Evelyn
spent the free days with us. In Venice we loved sitting in St.
Marks Square with Mildred and Evelyn listening to violins as
the sun set. We rode in a gondola and enjoyed shopping
and exploring beautiful churches together. We took a train
back to Bologna the next day. On the last day we took a
train to Ferrara and explored a large castle and cathedral.
We loved our trip to Italy and the wonderful meals and
excursions with such good friends.

In June there was a college retirement luncheon where President
Smith made more complimentary comments about Mildred and
me. He presented each of us with a beautiful Wagner chair and
kissed us good-by. The registrar's office took us out to dinner.
Ann Dillon gave me two lilac bushes, something I had always

wanted. The registrar's office also gave a party for us and we were presented with watches from the provost. All my friends who helped me with the awards dinners came and we took lots of pictures. My favorite student from my learning community, John Lanza, also came with a gift. He suffered from seizures and was legally blind, but he kept up with all the readings by enlarging them on the computer. He was one of the best debaters in class discussions and received straight A's in all his exams. I was so proud of him.

My last day at Wagner was to be June 30th. I worked furiously to get everything done before I left. On Friday, June 22nd, I decided to work until 10 or 11 p.m. Mike called me and said that we were going out to dinner and a movie. I told him that I had to work late. He became very insistent that we go out because Friday night was always "our night" on the town. I said no again and a little later he called to say that he had made reservations for dinner so I would have to come home. I thought, "Oh well, if it means so much to him I'll go home on time." When I drove up the driveway at home he came out to meet me. I said, "Well, get in the car and let's go to the restaurant." He told me to come in the house while he got the movie schedule, so I followed him. When I entered the front hall I heard, "SURPRISE!" I nearly fainted. I was stunned as I looked up and saw about 50 people in the living room.

Mike and the children had organized a magnificent surprise party for me. I kept asking him how the house got so clean and he said he had cleaned it himself and washed all the windows. Then he told me that our children had prepared the food, even Cindy who had flown in from Seattle. He pointed to the stairs to the living room and said, "There she is." She was sitting right in front of me and I hadn't seen her because I was in shock. I burst into tears and hugged her tightly. Then I looked around and saw all the people in the registrar's office and Judy Lunde from the president's office, and my favorite faculty, and the Deipnos and so many other wonderful friends. What a grand finale to all my years at Wagner that was.

Soon after I retired, President Smith left Wagner and took a position as president of the American International University in London. I was asked to speak at his farewell party. A new presidential search committee was formed at Wagner and Dr. Guarasci was voted in as the new president of Wagner College in 2002.

15

Nuptials

While Mike and I were pursuing our professional careers our family life continued to be active and exciting in the last decade of the century. We continued to enjoy movies and dancing on Friday nights and often on Saturdays too. We both exercised regularly, I with my swimming and walking, and Mike with his Nordic Track and tennis or racquetball. In June of 1990 Cathy was ordained as a Congregational minister in the Ponckhockie Church in Kingston, New York. The Deipnos came with us to the ordination and reception afterwards and we were all very proud of her. Marion McCreary wrote about the ordination in her weekly column in the *Bound Brook Chronicle.*

The next month we attended another ceremony that involved Cathy. She was invited to give the invocation at a session of the United States Senate. My father and brothers came with us to hear her. Before she spoke Senator Simpson of Wyoming, the senate whip, introduced her and told the audience that he was a very good friend of her Aunt Mary and Uncle David. Following the Senate session Senator Simpson took us on a tour of the senate and showed us his office. Then he treated us to lunch in the senate dining room.

In early August David and Mary spent a week with us at
Rockport. We celebrated Mike's 58th birthday on August 4th
and David's 60th on August 5th. The following week Mike, Steve,
Pete and some of their friends tore down the huge front porch
of our Rockport house and replaced it with a brand new one.
Pete and Steve really enjoyed the challenge. As they worked
Steve quizzed Pete constantly on what musical group was
playing on the radio. Steve knew them all but Pete kept asking
him for another hint. The new porch was gorgeous when they
finished and we took a picture of all the workers together, which
Peter has proudly displayed in his dining room ever since.

We made two trips to San Antonio that year, one in January and
the other in December to celebrate Dad's 90th birthday. Dad
reserved a private room for his party off the main dining room
at their retirement home, USAA Towers. He and Helen invited
close friends from the Towers, plus Dad's children and their
spouses, for a jolly party. We were surprised to find out that a
number of Helen's and Dad's friends from the Towers were closer
to our age than to theirs.

During December we attended many parties. Wagner's president
had been giving elegant Christmas parties at his rented presidential
mansion. At the November meeting of administrative heads he
had suggested that we change the location of his Christmas
parties to the college cafeteria. He asked the group what they
thought of the idea and no one answered him. So I piped up
and said that I thought he should continue to have the party in
his home as it was an enchanting atmosphere and everyone
seemed to enjoy the parties there. He looked at me and said "If
Connie likes our house better then we shall continue to have
the parties there." From then on he always reminded me as I
said good-by after the parties that I was the reason that he
continued to have them in his home. In addition to attending
the president's party in December, we also attended holiday
dinner dances sponsored by the Chamber of Commerce, the

Rotary Club and Center School and entertained the church couples group for the annual Progressive Christmas Dinner.

At the beginning of 1991 we were saddened by the death of our dear friend Ella Handen. Her husband, Jack, had died two years before. I was asked to give a eulogy for Ella at her funeral service and again at Bloomfield College where she taught for over 30 years. Ella and Jack had been two of our closest friends and had spent the July 4th weekend with us in Rockport for many years. We had attended plays at McCarter Theater in Princeton together for years with season tickets and always enjoyed a snack together afterwards. We also went on a number of bicycle trips with the Handens. Their daughter, Debbie, was Cindy's best friend all through school. Both girls were four years old when we moved next door to the Handens in 1962.

There were also happy occasions in 1991. A number of our relatives were married that year. Two children of my cousin Bob, Jimmy and Patsy Willing, were married in Massachusetts and our niece Nancy Smith was married in Wyoming. We attended all these events and thoroughly enjoyed them. Nancy wore her mother's wedding dress, which I remembered from 38 years before when I was a bridesmaid in Mary and David's wedding. Nancy married David Mooers of Houlton, Maine. Their reception was held under a tent at Nancy's parents' ranch on the South Fork of the Yellowstone River, thirty miles outside of Cody. We met Senator Simpson again at the reception and saw many of our relatives and Rockport friends there.

The next year, 1992, was the beginning of big celebrations in our family. On May 5th I was 60 years old and Beverly Weber threw a big party at her house with a three-piece band, which played our favorite dance tunes. She invited all of our family and many friends and served an elegant sit-down dinner to everyone. After my birthday a number of weddings occurred. In June our niece, Becky, married her high school sweetheart,

Bill Joyce. They were a handsome couple and had delightful personalities as well. They loved to play games, so every time we met together, we had fun with them. Their wedding was held in Rockville Maryland and our whole family attended. The DJ at the reception played good dance music and also led the young people in special dances. We all had a great time. The newlyweds settled in Seattle where Bill went to work for Microsoft. In September Mildred Nelson invited us to the wedding of her niece, Arti, in Boulder Colorado. She insisted on paying for our plane fare and hotel room in appreciation for her many visits to Rockport. The wedding was held out of doors facing a mountain covered with golden aspen. The reception was held next door in a hall that also looked out at the mountain. It was a lovely affair and Arti looked radiant next to her six-foot-five groom, Josh. Mike and I toured the state capitol the next day, something that he liked to do in every new state that we visited. We also enjoyed touring the campus of the University of Colorado where my brother Bunkie graduated.

In the fall of 1992 a series of weddings began for our four children. I had bemoaned for years the lack of a wedding among our children and feared we might never have any grandchildren. Then all four children were married one after another and grandchildren began to arrive. The first of the children to marry was Cindy. She met Denis Lavoie at Lotus Development Corporation in the fall of 1988. She admired him from the start, but they didn't start dating until the next spring. In the fall of 1991 Denis accepted a job with Asymetrics Corporation in Seattle. Our whole family knew how much Cindy liked Denis and we were all hoping that he would propose to her on her birthday before he left. When Cindy told us that Denis had given her a beautiful big bowl for a present, we were all disappointed, as we hoped it would be a ring.

Cindy flew to Seattle to spend Thanksgiving with Denis and in February she joined him for a ski weekend in Denver. Denis came back east in June for Becky and Bill's wedding. After the wedding he took Cindy on a trip to New England where he proposed to her in the woods of Monhegan Island just off the coast of Maine. They set the wedding date for October 4th in Rockport. Before Denis returned to Seattle he and Cindy found and reserved an ideal location for the reception. It was a spacious old mansion that originally belonged to the Tupper family and had been acquired by Endicott College as part of their program in hotel management. The mansion had a view of the ocean and several large rooms on the first floor where the reception would be held. There was a classic curved stairway on which to take a formal picture of the bride and groom.

Cindy was our first child to get married and I think that Mike and I were almost as excited as she and Denis were. We had a wonderful summer with Cindy at Rockport planning the wedding. She was living and working in Cambridge and came to Rockport almost every weekend where we discussed the wedding plans at breakfast, lunch and dinner. We often went to town and sat over coffee discussing menus and other details of the wedding. Caroline, her maid of honor, and Denis' sister, Celeste, came to Rockport one weekend to help Cindy address the wedding invitations. Cindy thought that it would be helpful for the guests if we listed some bed-and-breakfast spots for them to chose from. She and I had a great time visiting over a dozen inns. She made a list with a description and price list of each place and enclosed it, with a hand drawn map, in each wedding invitation. The women in Denis' family gave a wonderful bridal shower for Cindy and she was surprised and touched by it.

During the summer I visited a number of potential caterers for the reception. Most of them were too expensive. Finally I asked a cousin, Jeanette McDowell, to recommend a caterer and she suggested Gina in Manchester. As soon as I met Gina I was sold. She ran a tiny coffee shop and also a catering service.

She was inexpensive compared to the others that I had interviewed and I loved her personality. I told her that I wanted plenty of shrimp and that they should be served throughout the reception. She promised to see to my wish, and as the bride and groom left at the end of the reception, she passed me with a platter of shrimp and a smile saying, "Just as you requested."

Cindy and I went shopping together for her wedding dress. We went to a bridal shop in the Burlington Mall. She tried on one dress that did not suit her and then tried on the dress that we both fell in love with. It was a simple white cotton dress with a boat neck, lace bodice and long sleeves, and a full skirt with a big bow in the back. She looked just like my mother in that dress and, as she stood there smiling at me, I started to cry because she was so beautiful. She wore my mother's pearls and small pearl earrings. She was the loveliest bride I had ever seen.

Cindy and Denis asked Cathy to perform the marriage ceremony. The rehearsal was held late Friday afternoon, two days before the wedding. The rehearsal was confusing, but people assured us that it was a good omen and that everything would run smoothly at the wedding. This proved to be true. Denis' father told Denis that he would try to keep his wife from giving too much advice. We could see him restraining her several times during the rehearsal. On Friday evening Denis' parents hosted the rehearsal dinner at Peg Leg Restaurant in Rockport. It was a charming affair and the food was delicious. After dinner we went back to our house and watched Cindy and Denis open some gifts and then played round-robin ping-pong.

On Saturday the day before the wedding, we held a big picnic on the rocks for all the out-of-town guests and their families. We were lucky with the weather, which was warm for October. It was 80 degrees for the picnic and just a tad cooler for the wedding the next day with clear skies overhead both days. We hired a college student to cook at the picnic so that Cindy and

Denis would be free to socialize with their guests. Our family had prepared lots of food the day before and it was a successful picnic. It was so warm that my brothers and I went swimming off the rocks after the picnic. In the evening we had a pick-me-up supper and socialized with the relatives.

The wedding was on Sunday in the stately First Congregational Church in the center of Rockport. The bridal party wore long purple brocade dresses and carried purple and yellow flowers. Cindy's bouquet was made of yellow roses, purple iris and white daisies. The ushers looked handsome in their tuxedos, especially Peter and Steve. Steve ushered me to my seat and hugged me before I sat down. Mike escorted Cindy down the aisle, kissed her and presented her to Denis. Denis was beaming in his gray cutaway tuxedo as he took Cindy on his arm. Cathy performed the marriage ceremony perfectly and made some lovely comments about the love that Cindy and Denis shared. As Cindy and Denis marched out at the end of the ceremony they were glowing with happiness. The receiving line was held on the front lawn of the church and then Cindy and Denis were driven to the reception in a white Rolls Royce.

The reception was a huge success, thanks to Gina. There were three stations where different types of food were served. The back patio had a large assortment of appetizers. There was another station in the library, where an abundance of fruit and other foods were displayed. The Deipnos, including the Longs from Atlanta, sat at a table in the library surrounded by books and succulent food, a most appropriate setting for them. The third station of food was in the dining room where a sumptuous dinner was served buffet style. Filet mignon, ham, chicken, fish and all kinds of vegetables and salads were set out for the guests to select from.

A large ballroom separated the library from the dining room. A band played dance music in one corner of the room and tables and chairs were set up at the other end of the room where guests could eat and watch the dancing. Our family enjoys dancing and we were on the dance floor frequently. Waiters continually passed jumbo shrimp and other hors d'oeuvres. Gina had made a magnificent three-tiered chocolate cake with white frosting, decorated with purple and yellow flowers. When she brought the cake out to the middle of the dance floor to be cut, the band struck up a waltz and we all started dancing. Gina looked very nervous as the dancers twirled around the cake. After the dance, the band played the cut-the-cake song and Cindy and Denis made the first cut. Gina breathed a sigh of relief as the cake was passed to the guests.

When the reception was over and Cindy and Denis drove off we invited relatives and close friends back to our house in Rockport. My cousin Bob, whose summer home is next to ours, graciously offered us the use of his house because it had baseboard heating and the weather had turned chilly in the evening. Gina gave us many leftovers to take home including a complete filet mignon. We took a big platter of spinach dip and bread to Bob's house for the guests to munch on while we played charades. We invited them over for breakfast at our house the next morning before they left. We parceled out as many leftovers as possible to guests to take home with them. Cathy took half of the wedding cake to serve at the church meeting in Rick's church.

The whole experience of the first wedding in our family was thrilling. Our friend, Marion McCreary, wrote an article about the wedding for the *Bound Brook Chronicle*. She wrote: "We had a magical weekend attending the wedding of Cindy Schuyler, the daughter of Connie and Mike Schuyler of Bound Brook. The wedding took place at their summer home in the charming town of Rockport. The town, located on Cape Ann, is one of those beautiful places on the New England coast where you are awed when you arrive, and the kind of place to which you long to return. We picnicked on the massive flat rocks beside the ocean and watched the twin lighthouses on an island about a half a mile away. The lovely wedding was in the village Congregational Church . . ."

In the beginning of 1993 Cindy and Denis joined us for a visit to Dad and Helen in San Antonio, so that they could meet Denis. He charmed them both and we had a wonderful time together. We ate in the luxurious dining room in the USAA Towers and after dinner, when Dad and Helen retired, we took Cindy and Denis to our favorite country western dance hall. We took them to "Durty Nellie's" sing-along bar the second night. We all had a good time and they enjoyed meeting Dad and Helen.

Peter was our second child to get married. He met his future wife, Dorianne Sue Beckford, in August of 1991 when she became a tenant in his house in Annapolis, Maryland. When she moved in he was dating an athlete named Jackie. Peter brought Jackie to meet our family and we found her to be nice but aloof. Peter had a set of specific criteria for the woman he wished to have for a wife, the major one being that she must be an outstanding athlete with a great deal of stamina. He tested the stamina of his dates by hiking with them up a mountain and then taking them dancing when they came back down. Jackie fit that description of his "ideal" wife, but he hadn't considered other qualities that might make a good wife. When we met Dorianne at a picnic at Peter's house, we suggested that he look more closely at her if his relationship with Jackie didn't pan out.

In November Jackie and Peter broke up. In March of 1992 Dorianne accepted a date with Peter. They dated for a few months and then he gave her an even more challenging test than he had given other dates. He took her rock climbing and had her repel down a cliff. She managed to go through this terrifying ordeal with only a scratch on her ankle. She was relieved when she passed the test and vowed never to do anything like that again.

When Dorianne became romantically interested in Peter she moved out of his house. He took her mountain climbing in September and proposed to her. Her answer was, "This is the first time anyone asked me that," but she did not give him a definitive answer. In November he took her to Chincopeaque Island in Maryland where wild horses roam. They looked at rings together and apparently reached a mutual agreement about marriage. Dorianne's family invited Peter to spend Christmas with them that year. On Christmas morning he presented a small gift to Dorianne in front of her family. It was a diamond ring and he proposed to her as she opened it. After she said yes he asked her father for permission to marry her. They set a date of August 14, 1993 for the wedding.

Early in the summer before the wedding, we invited all of Dorianne's relatives to a picnic at Rockport. Dorianne is the youngest of seven children so a large number of relatives were at the picnic. We enjoyed meeting her parents, siblings, in-laws and cousins and the weather was perfect for the occasion. The Beckfords gave Dorianne a lovely bridal shower as the time of the wedding drew near. It was held at the home of Dorianne's oldest sister, Dianne, in Bradford Massachusetts. Steve and his girlfriend, Janice, were at Rockport at the time so Janice came with me to the shower.

Peter took charge of planning the wedding reception. My cousin Bob offered to let Peter use his yard at Rockport for the occasion. Until a couple of years before, the area between Bob's house and the ocean—a couple of acres—was covered with bushes and high grasses. Bob had recently cut down all the bushes, brought in loads of topsoil and created a spacious lawn. This made a perfect site for an outdoor reception with a magnificent view of the ocean and Straitsmouth Island. Peter accepted the offer with delight, as his finances were limited. He approached Gina to cater the wedding, but her price was a bit high for his budget, so he found a delicatessen to supply the food and cater the reception. He rented a large tent, which could cover 160 guests and a band. He also borrowed a smaller tent from the Naval Academy, where he was an associate professor and the assistant wrestling coach. He used the second tent to cover the buffet and bar tables.

Peter decided to make centerpieces for each table. He asked Steve to help him make 16 miniature lobster traps, one for the center of each table. During my walks on the beaches each evening during the summer I collected seashells to glue onto the lobster traps. They were unique centerpieces and many people commented on them. Peter wrapped the tent poles with pink crepe paper and set potted pink begonias around each pole. There was a large dance floor and Peter and Dorianne were seated at their own table in front of the dance floor.

On Thursday evening before the wedding Mike and I invited relatives from near and far to come to a picnic on the rocks. My brothers and their children were there as well as the Beckfords and Dorianne's maid of honor, Mary. It was good to catch up on family news and enjoy the spectacular sunset. On Friday evening Cathy conducted the rehearsal at the church in Bradford. When the wedding party had rehearsed the whole service several times and had done it all correctly, Peter insisted on doing it again to ensure that each participant knew what to do. Everyone groaned, but as usual, Peter had his way.

Mike and I had driven to Haverhill earlier in the summer to find a location for the rehearsal dinner and had found a lovely banquet room on the second floor of a new restaurant. After the rehearsal the wedding party and their spouses gathered at the restaurant for dinner. The tables were arranged in the shape of a "U" so that everyone could see all the guests. The bridal party included Dorianne's four sisters, her maid of honor, Mary, and Cindy. Peter's ushers included Dorianne's two brothers and Peter's friends from high school and college. Steve was his best man. Peter's and Dorianne's parents and Cathy, the minister, were also there. We filled the room completely. The dinner was tasty and everyone at the head table was asked to relate a story about his or her relation to the bride or groom. Peter and Dorianne also talked about their backgrounds and it was quite emotional at times.

The wedding was held in the First Congregational Church in Bradford on Saturday, August 14th. Dorianne's dress was beautiful. It was off the shoulder white brocade with a tiny waist and full skirt ending in a long train. She wore a long veil attached to a sparkling tiara on her head. Her bouquet was long and full of pink and white roses. The bridesmaids wore bright rose-colored brocade dresses with thin straps over the shoulders. During the ceremony they wore matching jackets with white lace trim. They carried rose-colored lilies in their bouquets. Peter wore a black cutaway tuxedo and he and Dorianne made a handsome couple. Cathy performed another inspirational wedding ceremony and Dorianne and her sisters cried during much of the ceremony. Peter chose "How Great Thou Art" as one of the hymns and I thought of God's greatness in bringing these two wonderful people together. After the ceremony there was a receiving line on the village green across from the church and then everyone drove to Rockport for the reception.

At the reception the food was ample and tasty. Our family had made a huge fruit salad to accompany the food that the caterer brought and there were generous portions for everyone. Dorianne's family brought a splendid three-tiered wedding cake. It was placed next to Peter and Dorianne on the side of the dance floor and after some boisterous dancing on the floor, the cake began to lean. Mike found some string and tied one of the pillars on the cake to a leg on an adjacent table, which kept it upright. Dancing was popular with the crowd and Dorianne's father, who is usually quiet and serious, led the chain dance with an engineer's hat on his head. Everyone enjoyed dancing to the song "Shout" and, from the oldest to the youngest, guests were throwing their arms into the air and yelling "shout, shout, shout." Relatives and friends of both the bride and groom were there along with many of Peter's wrestling friends. The Beckfords assembled for a family picture and the photographer had a hard time fitting everyone in. The pictures from the wedding were spectacular with sailboats on the ocean in the background. Pete and Dorianne flew to Newfoundland for their honeymoon. A week later they came back to Rockport and we all watched them open the gifts that had been left at the house.

After Peter's wedding Mike decided to put baseboard heating in our dining room at Rockport, as it had been so nice to enjoy a warm room at Bob's house after Cindy's wedding. He installed it on the two outside walls of the room. What a difference it made in the fall each year after that. We began hosting big dinners at the Rockport house in the fall, after the heating was put in, and we stayed well into October before closing the house for the winter.

In November Mike's dad became ill. Mike went down to San Antonio to be with him for ten days. I joined him at the end of his stay. Dad died on December 8, 1993, just short of his 93rd birthday. Our family flew down for the funeral service. Peter, Steve and their two male cousins were pallbearers at the service where Dad received a seventeen-gun salute. He was the senior four-star general in the United States Army at the time of his death. At the funeral service Mike gave a moving eulogy for his father. Our nephew, Hal Saxby, also paid tribute to him.

The beginning of 1994 was one of the coldest winters on record. It was so miserable that I suggested to Mike that we drive down

to the restored Baltimore harbor for the weekend of January
15th. We didn't get away from the cold, but we had a great time.
The temperature in Baltimore was zero degrees and we had to
buy mittens and hats to walk outdoors. We had a ten-block
walk from our hotel to the harbor and we were the only people
on the streets. We stayed at the Tremont Plaza Hotel, which was
charming. The accommodations were all suites, each with a
living room, dining room, stocked kitchen, bedroom and
bath. There was a delicatessen on the first floor so it was
easy to fill the refrigerator. We were so thrilled with our
suite that we called Peter and Dorianne in Annapolis and
invited them for cocktails after which we took them out to
dinner. On Saturday night Mike and I went to dinner and
dancing at the Hyatt Hotel overlooking the harbor. On
Sunday it snowed and we walked through drifts down to the
harbor to visit the Aquarium, one of the largest we had ever
seen. That night when we left there was a severe ice storm,
so we had a precarious drive home. We learned the next day
that Steve and Janice were driving up the New Jersey
Turnpike in the same storm on their way back from a trip to
Florida.

Our third child to get married was Steve. He met his bride to
be, Janice Kargol, on New Years Eve in 1991. They dated for
two and a half years before they married on June 12, 1994.
Janice had already shared in several Schuyler family
celebrations—my 60th birthday and Cindy's and Peter's
weddings—before marrying into the family, so we all felt close
to her even before Steve proposed to her. Steve proposed to
Janice at our house in Bound Brook. He had come over to see
Peter and Dorianne and Janice was to meet him there. She was
standing in the family room with Steve, Peter and Dorianne
when Steve looked at her and asked, "Do you want to get
married?" She said, "Yes." Steve's proposal might not have been
as romantically prepared as Denis' and Peter's, but it came from
the heart and Janice was thrilled. So were we.

A week after Steve's proposal, Mike and I took Janice to lunch and she had already bought her wedding dress. Janice's mother, Susan Kargol, gave her a splendid bridal shower. Mrs Kobezak, our beloved baby sitter for many years, was one of the guests. She was a friend of Janice's mother in Manville. I met another woman there who was the mother of one of Peter's high school wrestling rivals from Manville. She told me that her son had defeated Peter in high school and I told her that he did not, as Peter was undefeated in high school. We got into quite an argument and I'm sure Janice was wondering what kind of a mother-in-law she was getting. It turned out that the mother, Mrs. Specian, had mistaken Peter for another Bound Brook wrestler that her son had defeated, so the argument was peacefully resolved.

Mike and I gave a rehearsal dinner for Janice and Steve at Jaspers Restaurant on Friday night before the wedding. We reserved a private room with a large table and the food was excellent. Janice's matron of honor, Gloria, and her husband were there, as well as her brother, John, and his girlfriend, Heidi, Peter, Dorianne, Susan, Mike and I. It was a small intimate dinner that gave us a chance to know one another better. We felt that the dinner helped Gloria to feel comfortable in bringing her twins to the picnic the next day. The twins had such a good time that they didn't want to leave the picnic

We were worried about having a picnic in our yard, without the scenic rocks and ocean that we had at Rockport, but it turned out to be the best picnic yet. We put up tents and guests sat at tables under the tents and enjoyed talking with one another and watching the children play. Our niece Heather did a great job of leading games for the children and they really warmed up to her. We bought a play castle for the yard, put new chains on the swings and painted the lawn swing for the occasion. The small children enjoyed playing in the castle and even Uncle Ed was seen sliding down the little slide on the castle.

Mike's sister, Shirley, came with Ed, their four children and spouses, plus several grandchildren. All of my brothers came with most of their children and the Deipnos and many friends also came. We hired two high school students to grill the chicken and hamburgers and we prepared lots of other food. Beverly Weber volunteered to make the dessert and, in fact, she made twenty desserts, each one superb. My brother David, who loves sweets, said that he regretted he managed to sample only one half of the different delights, but he was in heaven.

At the end of the picnic our four children stood up and said that they had an important announcement to make. They asked Mike and me to come forward and announced that we would be celebrating our 40th wedding anniversary in four days. They said very complimentary things about us and told us that they wanted to give us a trip to celebrate our anniversary. They had made a big poster with the highlights of our marriage and pictures of five possible places for us to chose for our celebration. The choices included trips to Disney World, Santa Fe, New Orleans, San Diego or Alaska. We chose the cruise to Alaska and were excited and grateful to them.

Steve and Janice were married the next day by Cathy under an arbor outside the Pheasant Landing Restaurant where the reception was to be held. Janice's wedding dress was elegant. It was a white taffeta off the shoulder V-necked dress that looked becoming with her deep tan. The bodice and long sleeves were covered with heavy white lace blending into a full skirt with a long train. She wore a headpiece of small white flowers with buds cascading down her long brown hair. She carried three large white orchids with smaller orchids flowing down from them. She looked stunning. Gloria wore a pink satin dress under a white lace overdress with a pink satin bow in the back. She carried a bouquet of pink and white flowers. Steve and Peter looked very handsome in their tuxedos.

Cathy gave a sermon on love and talked of the love that Janice and Steve shared and could hope to nourish as they grew older. She said, "The friendship at the foundation of your love will serve you well. It will grow even as your love deepens, and as you each grow. Your future will be full of good times and hard times and passions of love, anger, ideas, joy and hope and more love." She told them. "Remember that your love needs your effort—effort to care, effort to support, effort to be concerned about one another's lives, effort to be honest about your dreams." She concluded, "And remember that your love is God's gift to the two of you. May this gift always cause you to look across the dinner table and say, this is my beloved and this is my friend."

The receiving line was held on the lawn outside the restaurant; then the wedding party and the guests moved inside and sat at assigned tables. An excellent meal was served and there was lots of dancing. A number of the guests were Bound Brook friends, such as Mary Parenteau and Ann Trombadore, who did not make it up to Rockport for the previous weddings. Mrs. Kobezak was there and all the children were delighted to see her. Cindy and Dorianne were both pregnant with their first children and had that glow that one sees so often on pregnant women. Cathy's beau, Rick Edwards, came late and she was impatient until he arrived. They had a great time dancing the rest of the evening after he came. Peter gave a moving toast as the best man. He talked of how Steve had always been his role model and how he looked up to him. He wished Steve and Janice much happiness. The reception ended with Steve and Janice cutting the four-tiered cake and Janice throwing the bouquet, which was caught by Heather.

After the reception Steve and Janice came to our house and opened gifts with all the relatives watching. The next morning they flew to Cozumel, on the Atlantic coast of Mexico. They stayed at a charming resort in their own little hut by the sea.

They went diving, their favorite sport, and took many gorgeous underwater photos. They returned tanned and happy with scores of slides and pictures to show us.

In July Mike and I went on a fabulous cruise to Alaska, the generous anniversary gift that our children had given us. We flew out to Seattle and spent the night with Cindy and Denis on July 23rd. The next day they drove us to Vancouver to board the Golden Princess ship. We were on the cruise for a week and we had a blast! We went on a number of expeditions outside the cruise ship including: white water rafting in Juneau, flying low in a four seat plane over glaciers in Skagway, riding a train over the Yukon Pass, watching glaciers break up in Glacier Bay, visiting a salmon hatchery in Ketchikan and riding on a small boat into the wilderness north of Ketchikan. I found it interesting that they spoke of glaciers "calfing" when big pieces of them broke loose and fell into the water. Cindy was much amused when we returned with photos from a complete roll of film showing tiny specks up in trees, the result of Mike's attempt to take a picture of a bald eagle.

During the cruise we sat with the same three couples for all of our meals. We met for the first time on the opening night of the cruise and we became fast friends immediately. One of the couples investigated all kinds of activities for us to enjoy on the days that we were cruising. It was fun to have friends to do things with. Mike and I capped off every evening with dancing in the Skylight Lounge. We spent one morning in the ship library each writing thank you letters to our four children for treating us to this wonderful experience.

When we returned we had a number of guests at Rockport. We invited another group of Wagner faculty who taught in the MDS program and had a grand time walking to town, picnicking on the rocks and playing *Trivial Pursuit* and round-robin ping-pong with them. They found a shack on

Bearskin Neck in town where one could purchase fresh lobsters off the boat and eat them on a deck that was built out into the harbor. We sat on crates and devoured lobsters gleefully. Beverly Weber, her sister, Barbara, and Millie Sheehan spent a week with me at Rockport, as they did every summer. Mildred Nelson and her niece, Evelyn, had also spent a week with me in June, as was their custom.

On August 16th our first grandchild, Sarah Marie Schuyler, was born to Peter and Dorianne. Dorianne went through 36 hours of labor and begged for a Caesarian section, but finally delivered Sarah naturally. Mike and I drove down to Annapolis as soon as possible to see our first grandchild. Sarah was, and still is, beautiful. In September my father had his 90th birthday. We gave him a party at his favorite restaurant and his great grandchild, Sarah, was there, as well as all his children and many of his grandchildren.

On November 22nd Thomas Schuyler Lavoie was born to Cindy and Denis. I was so excited when Cindy called me at work. I planned to fly out to see him on Thanksgiving, the earliest date for which I could get plane tickets. Cindy called us back the next day to tell us that the doctors thought something might be wrong with Thomas and they planned to keep him in the hospital longer. I flew out when Thomas was brought home and saw him for the first time curled up in the corner of his crib fast asleep. He was adorable. That night he woke Cindy at 3:00 a.m. screaming. Cindy was upset that she could not calm him down. In the morning she called the pediatrician's office to tell them of the incident and was told to bring him in for his appointment that afternoon. Cindy had an appointment that morning with her obstetrician so she left me with Thomas while she went to her doctor. Thomas began to cry so I tried to give him a bottle, which he refused to drink. I noticed that he looked blue around his lips. A little later his breathing became labored and he made a squeaky noise as he breathed. I called the pediatrician's office again and got the same response that Cindy had received earlier that morning.

When Cindy came home we drove to the pediatrician's office. In the waiting room Thomas' skin began to look gray, so we told the nurse and she took him in to see the doctor. The nurse tried to give him oxygen from two different canisters, both of which were empty. The nurse then picked up Thomas and declared, "We are not waiting another minute, I'm taking him to the emergency room!" She, Cindy and I ran through the halls to the emergency room in the hospital, which was attached to the office building. The doctors there gave Thomas oxygen immediately and called in a team from Seattle's Children Hospital. This team rushed him over to Children's Hospital and took him immediately to the Intensive Care Unit (ICU).

Cindy called Denis and he met us at Children's Hospital. We were ushered in to see Dr. Kawabori, a heart specialist for children. He told us that Thomas was in critical condition. He had a serious congenital heart deformity and his circulation was so compromised that his kidneys had shut down and his other major organs were also threatened. He told us that if the doctors could not stabilize Thomas' condition in the next 24 hours they would be unable to operate on him to save his life. All we could do was wait and pray. Cindy and Denis were devastated. They were allowed to sleep at the hospital to be near Thomas. I drove back to their house and prayed all the way home. I called Mike to tell him what was happening and continued praying. I eventually fell into a fitful sleep. The next day we were told that the doctors had been able to stabilize Thomas' condition and his kidneys were working again. He was scheduled for open—heart surgery. His diagnosis included coarctation of the aorta, and atrial and ventricular septal defects.

Denis is an optimist and an activist. He read about surgery for Thomas' congenital heart defects. He made little black and white mobiles for Thomas' incubator as he had read that newborns could distinguish black and white best. He and Cindy made an audio-tape of lullabies and other baby songs that they sang to Thomas. They put it in the corner of his incubator and the nurses played it to him. Denis learned that my Uncle Bob was a renown pediatric anesthesiologist, so he mentioned this to Thomas' anesthesiologist, who knew of him. Denis felt that the more influence he could bring to bear on the people who would be caring for his son, the better.

Thomas underwent open-heart surgery to correct his congenital heart defects. Dr. Lupenetti, the surgeon who operated on him, had developed a new technique for correcting coarctation of the aorta and it worked well on Thomas. He ligated the patent ductus and then cut the aorta on both sides of the narrowed lumen of the vessel. He enlarged both ends of the divided vessel and then reconstructed the aorta by anastomosis of the two ends. He corrected both the atrial and ventricular septal defects by sewing a knitted Dacron patch over each opening. The operation was a success and Thomas was completely cured. Cindy stayed with Thomas night and day for the month that he was recovering in the hospital. She pumped her breast milk for him while he was in ICU and when he came out of the incubator she was there to nurse him. Denis continued to be a tremendous support to her. I called Wagner College right after we found out about Thomas' diagnosis and told them that I was staying for an extra week to help out. I was so glad that I could be there with them.

January 1995 began with a horrible event. We received a phone call from Mike's sister, Shirley, telling us that her oldest grandchild, Michele, had been murdered. She was 18 years old and a freshman in college. Her high school sweetheart was murdered with her. They had been to a movie and drove out to a nearby park where he planned to give her a ring. While they were sitting in the car someone opened the door and shot her boyfriend and then her. The killer dragged Michele out of her door and shot her again. It was so shocking that it was almost unbelievable. She had been the valedictorian of her high school class and a star athlete. Mike and I immediately flew down to Georgia to be with her parents. Michele was the only child of Chris and Luis Cartagena, who adored her; Michele's boyfriend was also an only child. Michele was a beautiful young woman both in her looks and her personality. Michele's and her boyfriend's deaths were devastating to everyone who knew them. The murder was reported on the national TV program, *America's Most Wanted,* and this helped in the discovery of the murderer. He was the son of a sheriff who turned him in a few months later. This terrible event was devastating to all of the Saxby clan. Chris and Luis will probably never fully recover from this tragedy.

Mike and I flew to Seattle for the last week of January to see Thomas and celebrate a late Christmas with him and his family. Cindy cooked us gourmet meals all week except for one evening that we spent at the home of our niece Becky. Becky and Bill had become close friends of Cindy and Denis after they settled in Seattle. We played lots of games after dinner as we always did with Becky and Bill whenever we visited Seattle. On our way home from dinner I rode with Cindy, while Mike rode with Denis, as they had come in separate cars. Thomas started to cry loudly in the car and Cindy immediately pulled off the highway into a side street and nursed him. She said that whenever he cried hard she became terrified, after her original experience with his crying that had been so disastrous. We spent most evenings watching rented movies with Cindy and Denis at their home. Each evening either the men or the women would chose the video to rent and we enjoyed kidding each other over the good and "awful" choices. We took a trip into the mountains with Denis, Cindy and Thomas one day and ate lunch in a charming little German village. We had such a good time talking with them every day and hated to leave after only a week with them.

At the end of March Rick and Cathy called us and asked if they could come over for a visit. After they arrived we all went out to dinner in our car and Rick asked us for Cathy's hand in marriage. We were thrilled. When Rick met Cathy he was in the midst of divorce proceedings and was not yet free to marry Cathy. It took quite a while to sort out the provisions of the divorce, especially the visitation rights for his two daughters, Mary and Julie. He adored his girls and Cathy was also very fond of them. They were both exceptionally bright and talented. Each was at the top of her class and both were excellent singers and musicians. Julie was an outstanding ballet dancer and Mary was chosen for lead parts in her school musicals. Rick and Cathy were very proud of the girls' accomplishments and never missed a performance of either of them.

While Cathy was waiting for Rick's divorce to be completed she visited Atlanta, Georgia for six months to work and live in a shelter for the homeless. When her six months were up, she came to Hempstead, Long Island where Rick was pastor of the Methodist Church. She obtained a job in a drug store and moved in with a couple in Rick's church until she and Rick could get married. When the divorce was finally settled, Rick and Cathy immediately set a date for their wedding. Rick announced to his church on Palm Sunday that he planned to marry Cathy. He invited the whole church to attend their wedding. When he told them that the wedding date was in six weeks everyone was surprised and delighted.

In April Beverly Weber gave Cathy a bridal shower at her house. As always with Beverly it was an elegant affair with delicious food and many guests. Dorianne, Peter and Sarah were there as well as Mary and Julie and many friends. Sarah had a great time crawling under tables, scrunching wrapping paper and entertaining the guests. Cathy received many interesting and useful gifts. Mildred Nelson, who was also there, always gave extremely generous gifts to our children. She came to all their weddings and gave each one of them four complete place settings of the Lenox or Wedgewood china patterns that each couple had chosen. The women in Rick's church gave Cathy another bridal shower, where she received many elegant gifts such as crystal and china from her chosen patterns. One of the ladies in the church made her a splendid big cake for the occasion. I drove over to Hempstead from Wagner College to attend the shower. Cathy was not only surprised at the shower, but also at seeing me there.

Janice was pregnant and early in May her mother gave her a lovely baby shower. Janice and Steve's relatives and friends were there and Susan served a delicious repast in her charmingly decorated living room. Mrs. Kobezak was one of the guests and she presented Janice with many lovely handmade gifts. Susan had a beautiful big cake that she served at the end of the shower. Cathy arrived at the end of the party, but she stayed a while afterwards and enjoyed being with the family again.

On May 21, 1995 Cathy, our fourth and last child, was married. She and Rick held a picnic in the backyard of Rick's parsonage the day before the wedding. Many relatives and friends were there and, when it got dark, we all went inside and watched them open wedding gifts. The wedding was on Sunday. Cathy kept her wedding dress a secret and when I saw her come into the vestibule before going down the aisle I was stunned by the dress and how beautiful Cathy looked in it. The dress was white damask with a plunging "V" neck, small bows on each shoulder and big puffed-sleeves. It had a tight waistband that tied in a bow in the back. The skirt was full with a long train and Cathy carried yellow roses and lilies mixed with wild flowers. She wore a short veil clipped to the back of her head, which she removed as soon as the ceremony was over. Her college roommate, Yoshi, was her matron of honor and Mary, Cindy and Ashley, her best friend from seminary, were bridesmaids. Julie was a flower girl. Rick's friend Scott was his best man.

Cathy told the bridal party that they could wear any dress they owned as long as it was green, her favorite color. Mary and Julie wore new dresses; Mary's was green and Julie's was white with green trim. The bridal party all carried yellow lilies and purple wild flowers. Julie carried a small basket of pink roses.

Cathy and Rick were married by three of their best friends, all fellow ministers. After their declaration of marriage to each other, Cathy and Rick served communion to all the guests. It was a moving experience. We sat in the front row and it was fascinating to watch the guests as they came to the altar to receive communion. The receiving line was in the church parlor and, after going through the line, the guests moved into the church gymnasium where tables were set up and the band was seated on the stage ready to play. I had arranged for a five-piece brass band to play the music for dancing. The leader of the band, Bob Delfausse, was a fellow Wagner College professor who had taught in the MDS program for me. He had majored in liberal arts at Williams College, but he was also a very talented musician. I told him that we wanted lots of fast fox trots and waltzes and he obliged us splendidly. Thus we had still another wedding in the family with great dancing.

Our first two grandchildren, Sarah and Thomas, were at the wedding and Janice was expecting her first child shortly. Sarah crawled on the dance floor as much as she was allowed. Thomas loved dancing in his mother's arms and squealed with glee every time Cindy waltzed him around the floor. There was a big buffet in an adjacent room and the guests brought their plates back to the tables in the gym to eat their food. There was a three-tiered wedding cake and two extra oblong cakes on each side displayed on a table near the band. All the cakes were decorated with green flowers on white frosting. Cathy and Rick cut the cake at the end of the reception and Cathy threw her bouquet. The newlyweds spent their wedding night in the parsonage and the next morning Rick drove Julie and Mary back to their mother. He returned to Hempstead and took Cathy to the movies that night. They spent most of Tuesday packing and then drove to New Paltz to Mary's concert. Tuesday night they spent in a motel in Highland Falls and then drove to New York City on Wednesday morning. They spent the day in the city and the night at Union Theological Seminary. On Thursday they drove to New Paltz, picked up Mary and Julie and took them to Mohonk Resort with them for the rest of the week. Rick had been asked to be the Minister in Residence at Mohonk for the Memorial Day weekend so they were given rooms gratis during their stay. On Monday morning they returned the girls to New Paltz and went back to Mohonk for the rest of the day.

On June 23rd Mike and I spent four days in Cancun, Mexico at a GBS convention. We received a group rate for our room, which gave us a sizable reduction of the regular price. We stayed in a five-star hotel where all the rooms faced the ocean. Our room had a sitting room looking out to sea. We could see the people at the bar in the center of the pool below our window. It was very hot in Cancun, so I did not go outside the hotel until evening. I swam in the ocean from 6:00 to 7:00 p.m. every evening and the water was warm and wonderful. While Mike went to meetings I read in our sitting room and occasionally went to a small air-conditioned shopping mall across the street from the hotel. We ate our meals at the hotel, which had several first-rate restaurants. One day we took a bus into town and bought a hand embroidered dress for Steve and Janice's not-yet-born baby girl. It turned out to be her favorite dress for years. It was size four so it took her a while to grow into it, but it was the smallest one they had in the market. We thoroughly enjoyed Cancun and came home rested with happy memories.

16

The Next Generation

Mike and I had wondered for years if we would ever have grandchildren, but they finally began to arrive and they kept coming until we had eleven little ones and two older step-granddaughters. Sarah Marie Schuyler, the first grandchild, arrived on August 16, 1994. We drove down to Annapolis, Maryland to see her and she was beautiful. Her parents, Peter and Dorianne, had bought an attractive house in Annapolis when they married. It had a big living room, dining room and kitchen with an adjacent screened porch downstairs and three bedrooms on the second floor, so there was ample room for them and their growing family.

I started my first "Grandma's Album" when Dorianne gave me one for Grandparents' Day in September. It didn't take long to fill it. Photographing grandchildren became my favorite hobby. Each year I filled two large family albums. I also kept a small album of special pictures for each grandchild. In September Steve and Janice joined us on a drive to Maryland to see Sarah and we spent the night at Peter's house. The next day we all drove to Kensington, Maryland to celebrate my father's 90th birthday. Sarah was with us and we had a picture taken of the four generations. On the first of October we went to see Sarah again and saw the Navy football game with her and her parents.

After the game we returned to Peter's house for a picnic. The next weekend Dorianne drove up to Massachusetts with Sarah to visit her family in Haverhill. During her visit she brought Sarah to Rockport to see us. In November Dorianne and Peter invited all the relatives to Sarah's christening service and hosted a big reception afterwards at their house.

Thomas Schuyler Lavoie, Cindy and Denis' first baby, arrived on November 22, 1994. His harrowing experience with open-heart surgery a week after his birth had us all very worried, but he came through it all successfully. I stayed in Seattle for an extra week and after Thomas' condition stabilized I returned to Bound Brook, promising Cindy and Denis that Mike and I would return to celebrate Christmas with them after Thomas came home from the hospital.

Mike and I decided to celebrate Christmas with our children on December 26 so that they could spend Christmas day with their immediate families. Peter, Dorianne and Sarah joined us on that day along with Steve, Janice and Cathy. Sarah was only four months old, but Mike insisted on buying her a fire engine to ride on. Peter held her on the fire engine and pushed it with the siren wailing and the lights flashing. Sarah was delighted; she was so excited that her eyes nearly popped out of their sockets. After opening the gifts we sat down to a big roast beef dinner.

During the second week of January 1995 we visited Peter and Dorianne in Annapolis and my father in the hospital where he had undergone surgery on his gallbladder. My brother David had come from Wyoming to see Father also. After our visit to see Father, who was recuperating well, we ate lunch with David and Steve Smith. The next day we went back to Peter's house and babysat with Sarah that night. Sarah liked to move, so Mike and I marched around the downstairs singing marching songs to her. Barney, the family dog, joined the parade. Sarah didn't cry as long as we kept marching.

At the end of the month we flew to Seattle to celebrate a late Christmas with Cindy, Denis and Thomas. We all had dinner with our niece Becky and her husband, Bill, at their new house on our first night there and we played *Taboo*, their favorite game, after dinner. We celebrated Christmas on January 27, by opening gifts and sharing a delicious roast beef dinner. In the middle of dinner there was a mild earthquake to add to the excitement. On Sunday we drove to see Mount Rainier. We kept looking for it and then suddenly it appeared in the car window. It was an awesome sight. Cindy and Denis had climbed Rainer before they had children. They had to take lessons before actually ascending the mountain. They were told that if any of the climbers felt unable to continue the ascent, they would be tied to a tree to wait for the other climbers to return and untie them. This was done as a safeguard against the climber wandering off and getting lost. Thank goodness Denis and Cindy made it to the top without a problem. On Monday we went to see a spectacular waterfall and came back to enjoy Cindy's Chicken Kiev dinner at home. Each night we rented a film to watch with Cindy and Denis in their beautiful family room. I went back to Seattle for a week in March to see Thomas again. I sat with him a few times so that Cindy could get out. When I put him in his jump seat he kicked his feet with glee as he bounced up and down in it. He had a wonderful grin that covered his lower face, making everyone enjoy being with him.

After I returned home Mike and I visited Sarah frequently. Sometimes we took her and her parents to restaurants. We tried to keep her entertained while we waited for our meals as she had a habit of letting out piercing screams when she was bored. When this happened, Peter or Mike would take her out for a little walk. We usually visited my father when we went down to Maryland. He was becoming feeble and unable to care for himself. My brothers David and Bunkie came east to persuade Father to move to Kansas and live with Bunkie and his wife, Ann. He finally agreed and moved to Kansas where he seemed happy in their home. He loved Ann's cooking and he like to watch old movies, especially *It Happened One Night* and *Snow White and the Seven Dwarfs*.

When Father left Kensington, he told his children that he wanted them to distribute his belongings before his house was sold. My three brothers and I arranged to go to Father's house to divide up his furniture at the end of March after he had moved to Kansas. I went down a few weeks earlier to make an inventory of his belongings, which was sent to all his children and grandchildren. The grandchildren were more interested in acquiring furniture than his children, who already had enough belongings of their own. The grandchildren mailed their selection lists to their parents. When we got together, my brothers and I took turns selecting items for ourselves or for our children.

My first choice was a small picture of Rockport rocks that my Uncle Frank had painted for Mother. The rest of my choices were for our children. Steve and Cindy desired nothing. Peter selected a number of small tables, some bureaus and a large bookcase. Cathy chose the mahogany dining room set that originally belonged to my maternal grandmother. The set included a huge mirror that was too large to fit in Cathy's dining room. My sister-in-law Carol announced that she would like it for her living room. She said that it would remind her of my mother of whom she was very fond. She remembered how Mother could never resist looking at herself in that mirror as she brought food to the table. Cathy also chose one of the original paintings of a bromeliad that had been created for my Father's encyclopedia of bromeliads. The nicest aspect of our children's acquiring my parents' possessions is the opportunities it affords me to see cherished items whenever I visit them. David and Bunkie chose a number of beds and other furniture, rugs and utensils for themselves and their children. They transported their furniture out west in a U-Haul truck. Peter drove his furniture home to Annapolis the evening after we finished choosing, and the next day he drove a rented truck full of Cathy's selections to Bound Brook. Rick picked up her choices from our garage the following day.

After Cathy and Rick were married they settled into the parsonage. It was a lovely house with a big living room, dining room and kitchen, and a small den on the first floor. There were four bedrooms on the second floor. Rick's daughters Mary and Julie each had a room of her own. They lived with their mother during the week, but spent alternate weekends and some vacation time with Rick and Cathy.

After Mike and I returned from the GBS convention in Cancun in June we visited Rockport to celebrate the July 4th weekend. In the evening of July 2 we were reading in the living room when the phone rang at 11:30 p.m. We were sure that the call must be about Kristen's birth, so I ran to the phone and was overjoyed to hear the news of her arrival. We drove home the next day and went immediately to see Kristen. I adored her from the moment I first saw her. She lived close enough that we could see her regularly. She had a quiet sweet way about her that charmed everyone who saw her.

Sarah celebrated her first birthday at Rockport. We began a tradition of inviting Dorianne's parents and family, as well as our own relatives, to celebrate Sarah's birthdays at Rockport. She received many gifts and enjoyed sitting at the head of the big table while all the guests watched her open them. Her favorite present that year was a soft stuffed seal from her cousin Heather. She hugged the seal with glee and Heather was pleased to see how much Sarah appreciated her gift. Sarah took her first step the day after her birthday and everyone was very excited.

On Labor Day weekend we had our annual family reunion at Rockport. Saturday night the family attended a big picnic at the Gordon house. Emily Gordon, my best friend at Rockport, was the sister of Mary Smith, the wife of my brother David. Emily had five children and was acquiring grandchildren similar in age to our own grandchildren. We always shared picnics and parties between our two families during holiday weekends in the summer. The weekend included picnics on our rocks, lots of games, and delicious meals around our big dining room table. Thomas and Sarah had a great time together playing in the boat in the dining room and under the dining room table. They played in the pools at the rocks and enjoyed splashing together in the warm bathtub water afterwards. I took many pictures of the family that weekend filling up thirty pages in our big photo album. On the last night we showed home movies of our children when they were babies. Our children and their spouses got a kick out of seeing those old movies.

Mike and I had to go back to New Jersey to start work on Tuesday. Cindy and Denis stayed on at Rockport for another week. We returned to Rockport on Thursday night with Steve, Janice and Kristen. Because the weather could be a bit nippy in September, I bought two blanket sleepers, one bigger than the other, to keep baby Kristen warm. I took more pictures the second weekend. The ocean in September is a royal blue color and the leaves begin to change color, making a colorful scenic background for pictures. We sat around the dining room table eating hearty meals and sharing stories. Our children and their spouses were a great help and supplied us daily with eggs, bacon and croissants for breakfasts. Steve was our breakfast chef whenever he was at Rockport. Kristen was a happy baby all weekend and we had a great time together. For Saturday we invited Denis' siblings and their families to our house for dinner. Cindy and Steve were a big help in preparing dinner for such a big crowd. The Lavoie grandchildren and ours enjoyed playing together. On our last day Steve went diving and brought back several lobsters. We had a feast of turkey and lobsters to celebrate our last meal together. Mike and I continued to drive up to Rockport on weekends until

Columbus Day weekend when we closed the house for the winter. As always I had a hard time saying good-by to Rockport for another year.

In mid October, we invited Steve, Peter and Cathy and their families to dinner in Bound Brook. We also invited Ralph Pritchard, our best friend from our church. We had a grand time eating, talking and playing with the grandchildren. Sarah enjoyed riding on Peter's back and doing summersaults in the air holding on to her daddy's hands. A week later we were invited to dinner by Steve and Janice and, as usual, Janice cooked us a delicious meal. I took another bunch of pictures at both dinners. I was turning into quite a proficient photographer. Dinner with Steve, Janice and Kristen became a regular occasion in our lives and frequently Peter's family joined us. Steve's family came to our house for Thanksgiving, and on Christmas our whole family was with us. We opened gifts and shared a delicious roast beef dinner together. On Christmas night we all went to the Weber house to continue our long-standing tradition of joining together socially in the spirit of Christmas conviviality.

At the beginning of 1996 Mike and I decided to break away from the cold New Jersey winter to visit some idyllic spot in the sunny south. On the Martin Luther King holiday weekend we left Newark in a snowstorm and flew to Nassau where we stayed in a Holiday Inn on the ocean. We had a beautiful view from our balcony and could watch the cruise ships docking in the harbor. We bought two muffins at the hotel deli each evening and sat on our balcony in the mornings sipping coffee and munching on our muffins. I swam twice a day in the ocean cove next to our hotel while Mike read his book on the beach. We walked around the island and visited the grandiose Atlantis Resort next door to our little hotel. We enjoyed dinner and dancing at nearby restaurants and flew home thoroughly rested and happy after three days.

During the year Mike and I spent a great deal of time with our children and grandchildren. We regularly shared dinner with Steve, Janice and Kristen at both our homes and also at restaurants. They had purchased a large two family Victorian house in Clinton, New Jersey. They rented out the upstairs apartment and lived in the larger apartment on the first floor. Clinton is a quaint old town with many charming restaurants and shops. I frequently took care of Kristen on weekends. She had a cheerful disposition and I loved being with her. I was overjoyed when at eight months old, she said "Nana." As she was the first grandchild to call me by name, I decided that Nana would be my title from then on.

In April Mike was chosen as "Man of the Year" by the Bound Brook Chamber of Commerce. The Chamber hosted a dinner dance in his honor and we invited our best friends, Dick and Beverly Weber, as our guests. The President of the Chamber of Commerce read a moving speech about Mike, which appeared in the paper the next day. Our favorite band played wonderful dance music for us and we had a great time. We also celebrated Cathy's birthday that month and, in May, we took Cathy, Rick, Steve, Janice and Kristen out to dinner for Mothers' Day.

At the end of May we flew to Seattle to visit Cindy, Denis and Thomas. While we were there we visited our niece Sarah Perkins in Quilcene on the Olympic Peninsula. We took a ferry from Seattle to the peninsula and drove for about two hours to Quilcene. Sarah, her husband, Scott, and their three children lived in a yurt in the woods. The yurt was a huge prefabricated octagonal room with a kitchen and dining area on one side and a living area on the other. The neighbors had helped them erect the yurt and later Scott had built an addition of three bedrooms and a TV room onto the original building. The whole house was made of redwood and the back of the house looked out over the water. When we arrived, the family had been collecting shellfish all morning. They treated us to a feast and we had a great time visiting with them. Their three children, Elsie, Sally and Ezra, entertained us by standing on their heads on the couch. They liked Thomas and gave him their toys to play with.

The next day we visited the Woodland Park Zoo with Thomas and his parents. Becky and Bill came over for dinner and we played *Taboo* together afterwards. On our last day we drove north of Seattle to see fields of tulips in La Conner. It was like being in Holland in springtime. After returning from Seattle we attended a surprise party at Peter and Dorianne's house in Annapolis for Steve's fortieth birthday. Steve was truly surprised and thrilled to be so honored. My brother Steve and his family came over from Rockville to join the festivities.

I returned to Annapolis ten days later to stay with Sarah while Dorianne went to the hospital to give birth to Cortlandt. He arrived on June 21, 1996 at 2:47 p.m. Peter was present at the delivery, but the doctor was not especially pleased at his presence. Peter was afraid that the doctor was damaging Cortlandt's head and urged the doctor to treat him more carefully. The doctor kept reassuring him that the baby was not being hurt, but after a while, Peter got on his nerves. Peter called to tell me that the hospital would allow Sarah to visit her new brother. When Sarah and I arrived at the hospital the nurse gave me a form to fill out before we could go into Dorianne's room. While I was trying to fill out the form Sarah was running up and down the corridors. I finally finished filling out the form, retrieved Sarah and went into the room. Sarah was not overly pleased to see Cortlandt in Dorianne's arms. She demanded that her mother should come home with her and I didn't hear her mention that the baby should come too. A week later I returned to take care of Sarah while Peter and Dorianne took Cortlandt to Johns Hopkins for x-rays. Cortlandt had been born with only one functioning kidney. The specialist at Johns Hopkins advised them that the best method of dealing with a deformed kidney was to let it shrivel up and disappear rather than perform invasive surgery to remove it. They followed this advice and the deformed kidney disappeared. The doctor told them that people with only one kidney generally live long lives with no kidney problems.

Over the July 4th weekend we gathered again at Rockport for picnics, parades and fun. Kristen celebrated her first birthday at Rockport with a big family party. After Kristen was a year old Janice took a part-time job with *The Hunterdon Democrat* newspaper. She and Steve found a wonderful babysitter, Tara, to watch Kristen. Tara had a son, Andrew, about Kristen's age and they played well together. Steve and Janice were pleased with the quality of care that Tara gave Kristen and they became good friends with Tara and her husband, Dave.

The Hunterdon Democrat handled the advertising for the Hot Air Balloon Festival at Solberg Airport each year and the paper received free tickets for balloon rides. The paper held a drawing for their staff to get free tickets for balloon rides. Janice won two tickets and was thrilled. She and Steve went on a balloon ride while Janice's mother watched Kristen. Janice took marvelous pictures of all the balloons with her camcorder. The balloons were brightly colored with beautiful designs and there were a number of specially shaped balloons including a sneaker, a maple leaf, a dragon, a pizza, a birthday cake and the Planter's Peanut man. After the balloons landed Janice took pictures of the involved procedure of deflating the balloons and packing them into trucks. Purely by coincidence Mike and I were driving on Route 202 just as the balloons were landing in a field along the road. They came so low over the road that the traffic stopped and we could see the people in the baskets under the balloons. At that time we were unaware that Steve and Janice were in one of those baskets. We didn't see them but the next day they told us all about their ride. In subsequent years Steve and Janice invited us to the balloon festivals and we enjoyed joining them to watch the balloons take flight.

Mike and I flew to Las Vegas for a GBS convention at the beginning of August. We had a good time, as we always did on vacations together, but it was so hot that we could only go outside in the evenings. I swam daily in a fancy pool at Caesar's Palace where we stayed. The pool had statues of Roman leaders on each corner and luxurious plants bordering its sides, but it couldn't compare to swimming at Rockport. At the end of the week Mike flew back to New Jersey and I flew to Boston to spend a week with Beverly Weber and Millie Sheehan at Rockport. Beverly met me at Logan Airport and we drove to Rockport. It was dusk when we arrived, but I ran down to the rocks for a swim before the sun went down. As I swam and saw the seaweed turn to gold in the glow of the setting sun I felt that I was in an enchanted paradise. The water was cool and refreshing and I sang as I swam back and forth across the cove.

At the end of August Peter and his family moved to Flemington, New Jersey. He had not received tenure at the end of his seventh year at the Naval Academy and, unable to find a suitable coaching position elsewhere, he reluctantly left the field of wrestling and entered the business world. He found a job with Pennick-Aramour, a landscaping company in New Jersey and Pennsylvania. He and Dorianne moved into a town house in Flemington until they could find a house. Mike, Steve and I drove to Annapolis to help them move. No sooner had they arrived in Flemington than Sarah locked herself in the bathroom of her new home. Fortunately Steve had his tools with him, so he took the bathroom door off the hinges and we retrieved Sarah. The next calamity came when Sarah climbed up the ramp onto the moving van and fell off the truck onto the driveway. A lump the size of an egg appeared on her forehead. From then on, belatedly, we didn't let her out of our sight.

The entire family gathered at Rockport over the Labor Day weekend. It was a stormy weekend because of a hurricane that came up from the south. We walked down to the rocks with the

Gordon family to watch the mighty waves, then came back to the house to play games, watch the antics of the grandchildren and reminisce about past experiences over a hearty meal. We went back to Bound Brook on Monday night, but returned in a few days to spend another long weekend with the Lavoies before they returned to Seattle. We also attended Emily and Dick Gordon's 45th wedding anniversary dinner and celebrated Dorianne's birthday at the Rockport house that September.

Back in Bound Brook we alternated babysitting with Sarah and Cortlandt and with Kristen. I could manage Kristen alone, but it took both Mike and me together to manage Sarah and Cortlandt. Two years old at this time, Sarah was a beautiful little girl but was bursting with energy that she could not control. One time while we were caring for them I was feeding Cortlandt and I called out to Mike that Sarah was headed for the kitchen. Before Mike could catch up to her, Sarah pulled out a draw and threw all the silverware on the floor. A bit later I told Mike that Sarah was going upstairs. Before he caught up to her she had smeared Desitin on her bedroom walls. Later while I was answering the phone Sarah pulled her hand out of mine and raced across the living room to push Cortlandt right out of Mike's grasp into a dollhouse. All this occurred in one evening in their small town house in Flemington. Dorianne had her hands full with Sarah and Cortlandt. In October I received a call at work from her saying that she was taking Cortlandt to the hospital for a spinal tap. I rushed out of my office and drove to the hospital in Flemington so that I could watch Sarah while Dorianne was with Cortlandt. Fortunately the spinal tap revealed no disease.

We saw a great deal of Kristen. She loved music and she swayed to the tunes on the radio or TV. Steve nicknamed her "Quirmy Quirmo" and she enjoyed doing the "Quirmy Quirmo Boogie" on her parents' big bed. We frequently had dinner at her house or our house or went out to dinner with her family. She liked it when the waiters joined together to sing *Happy Birthday* to various customers in some of the restaurants. While we waited for our meals she and Mike frequently went for short walks or played hide and seek in the lobby.

We did not close the Rockport house early in October 1996 because Dorianne's nephew, Eric, was to be married on October 26th in Massachusetts and we planned to stay in Rockport with Pete and Dorianne that weekend. We hired my cousin's sixteen-year-old son, Nicholas, to sit with Sarah and Cortlandt while we were at the wedding and reception. Nicholas was six feet six inches tall and when Sarah saw him she was somewhat cowed by his size. We told Nicholas that he was never to take his eyes off of Sarah. We said, "Cortlandt is safely strapped in his seat so do not leave Sarah alone to go and tend to him if he cries. Take Sarah with you wherever you go."

We went to Eric and Christina's wedding and enjoyed ourselves immensely. Dorianne loved line dancing with her relatives and friends. When we returned to our house we asked Nicholas how he had managed. He said that he had heeded our instructions, but this required a bit of ingenuity. While he was giving Sarah a bath, Cortlandt began to cry downstairs. Sarah would not get out of the tub, so Nicholas hid behind the bathroom door. When Sarah couldn't see him she got out of the tub to look for him. Nicholas grabbed her with a towel and carried her downstairs to tend to Cortlandt's needs.

Cortlandt was christened in November and Peter and Dorianne gave another big christening party. In early December we celebrated Peter's birthday. We flew to Seattle a few weeks later to celebrate an early Christmas with Cindy, Denis and Thomas. Thomas was just two, an adorable little fellow with a big grin. He helped hang a few items on the Christmas tree and looked with wonder at all the pretty ornaments. He was small for his age but he had a voracious appetite. He could wolf down two giant bagels for breakfast every morning and enjoyed his other meals as well. Thomas received a car from Santa that he could sit in and squealed for joy as he drove around the house. He liked to throw balls and run after them when Denis threw them back. He was a happy child and we had a great time celebrating Christmas with him and his parents. On our last evening in Seattle Becky and Bill visited and we met their new baby girl, Amanda.

Our niece Heather was living in New York at the time and she joined us for Christmas as she could not afford to go home to Kansas. Heather enjoyed playing with the grandchildren on Christmas Day and holding baby Cortlandt. After Christmas we drove to Hempstead, Long Island with Peter's and Steve's families to celebrate Rick's birthday on December 29th. I also took part in Christine Hagedorn's wedding at the end of December. She worked for me at Wagner and we had become close friends. I read the New Testament passage at the ceremony. She was a beautiful young woman and looked radiant in her wedding gown. She had admired my Mike and had sought a sweet natured man like him for her own husband. Jeff Nordanholt fit her ideal as he was good natured, easygoing and adored her.

During the following year we continued our weekend dates of movies and dancing at Patullo's Tavern in Bound Brook. Herbie Patullo hired a two-piece band that played the kind of music we enjoy every Friday and Saturday and we rarely missed a weekend there. The band knew our favorite songs and played them whenever we were there. Throughout each week our spirits were upheld by the anticipation of our Friday or Saturday night movie and dancing at Patullo's.

Over the Martin Luther King weekend of 1997, Mike and I escaped from winter work for a vacation in Ft. Lauderdale and Nassau. I spent two days swimming at Ft Lauderdale while Mike read on the beach. The air temperature was in the low fifties, but the water felt wonderful. When I was ready to come out of the water I waved to Mike and he brought a big thick towel down to the water's edge so I could wrap up in it and not freeze. After my swim each day, we drove up the Florida coast and ate lunch and dinner at some of the elegant resorts along the way. After two days we boarded a cruise ship for a two-day trip to Nassau. The food on the ship was plentiful and delicious for me, but Mike was seasick and stayed in our room. Later he felt up to watching a movie. We docked at Nassau the next morning and took a small boat out to a tiny island off the coast of Nassau. We danced to calypso music on the boat and, when we reached the island, I swam to my heart's content. We came back to the ship for a sumptuous meal that night.

We continued to baby-sit and enjoy dinners regularly with Peter's and Steve's families through the winter and spring. Kristen and I began to go on little walks, as the weather became warmer in the spring. We walked from her house across the old bridge into the center of Clinton. We stopped to watch the ducks and geese in the river and the fishermen in their big boots standing in the water. I took pictures of Kristen standing on the bridge with the old mill and pretty waterfall in the background.

In April we gave a birthday party for Cathy at our house. Steve and Peter came with their families and Ralph Pritchard also came. The grandchildren had a wonderful time staging tea parties, hunting for plastic Easter eggs and singing their little songs such as *The Wheels on the Bus* and *Pat-a-Cake*. The parents kept telling them to hug each other, but the only child willing to do so was Sarah, who also delighted in carrying chairs around. We brought in a big cake for Cathy after dinner and the children all sang *Happy Birthday* to her. Later in the month we drove to New Paltz, New York to see Rick's daughter, Mary, play the lead role in her school play, *The Music Man*.

In May Mike arranged a surprise birthday party for my 65th birthday at Patullo's, the restaurant where we went dancing on weekends. The party was held in the garden room, which we had all to ourselves. The grandchildren loved running up and down the room and we all had a great time. We enjoyed it so much that we decided to make this an annual family affair. Janice's birthday is on May 10th and Mother's Day comes at the same time. Since that time we have enjoyed a big family celebration every year for Mother's Day and the two birthdays.

Mike and I flew to Seattle for the Memorial Day weekend to be with Cindy, Denis and Thomas. They entertained us royally as always. We took a ferry to the Olympic Peninsula and drove to the Fort Defiance Zoo. Thomas was interested in the variety of animals and fishes in the zoo. On our way back to the ferry we stopped at Never Never Land to see replicas of nursery rhyme characters. During our visit Becky, Bill and Amanda came to dinner one evening and on nights that we were alone with Cindy and Denis we watched movies together in the family room. On our last day we walked along the beach and threw the ball to Thomas on the way. We had such fun that we hated to leave.

When we returned home our niece Heidi called to ask us if her family could come to Rockport in June to celebrate her father's graduation from Harvard graduate school. He had been working on a doctorate for many years and finally finished it. We all loved Heidi, who had a "heart of gold", so we told her that they could stay at Rockport. The hit of the weekend was Heidi's two-year-old son, Wolfie. Kristen and her parents were also there and Wolfie and Kristen got along beautifully. We also enjoyed seeing Heidi's sister, Stephanie, and her boyfriend, Stan. We held a birthday party for our Steve at Rockport while they were there and we all enjoyed ourselves

After we returned to Bound Brook we attended a picnic to celebrate Cortlandt's first birthday. His cousin Kristen was

there as was Millie Sheehan, Beverly Weber and her young
grandson, Matthew. During the party Sarah reached into the
grill and picked up a glowing coal with her bare hand. We
immediately put her hand in cold water, then Dorianne
rushed her to the hospital. The guests went back to the house
for ice cream and cake and Dorianne returned with Sarah
whose hand was bandaged. Over the next few weeks the
burn healed completely, thank goodness. Although she was
under three years of age when it happened, Sarah remembers
the incident vividly.

Another sad event that month was my father's death. He was
93 years old and we held a memorial service for him in his
home church in Kensington, Maryland. His children wrote
memorials about him, which the minister read at the service.
After the service a reception was held in the church parlor,
then the relatives gathered at my brother Steve's house in
Rockville for dinner. Harvard University dedicated a 360-page
issue of *Harvard Papers in Botany* to Father entitled *A Tribute
to Lyman Bradford Smith (1904-1997)*. It contains several short
biographies of his life by his family and colleagues as well as
many tributes to different aspects of his work by other
colleagues. It lists his 519 publications and describes his life-
time research. It lists over 2700 plants that have been named
by him or in his honor, with many illustrations, some of which
I drew for Father's publications when I was a child. Included in
the book are many photos of him, his family and his colleagues.
It is an impressive memorial to him.

I spent most of July and half of August that year in Rockport.
Steve's family arrived for July 4th and Kristen's birthday.
Beverly and Millie came for one week and my brother Steve
and his wife, Carol, came for another week. Janice and Kristen
spent a week in August with me and we went to the beach every
day. I came back to Bound Brook in the middle of August and
gave a birthday party for Sarah at our house. The next weekend

I took Kristen to Belmar at the New Jersey shore to visit former members of the Deipnos, Gerry and Connie D'Alessandro, and their granddaughter Anna, who was the same age as Kristen. We had a wonderful time on the beach. I frequently went to Belmar to swim on weekends when I wasn't at Rockport, especially in the fall. I always stopped by Connie's house to have coffee and to chat with her after my swim.

On September 18th Janice's mother, Susan Kargol, died suddenly. Mike and I took turns sitting with Kristen during the viewing. After the funeral service, Janice invited her mother's friends and relatives back to her mother's house in Manville. Susan Kargol had worried that she would never have a grandchild, so when Kristen came into the world she brought her a great deal of joy. At the viewing, Janice put a small picture of Kristen in the coffin next to her mother.

Mike had been in charge of the Rotary Club's annual pancake breakfast for several years. The Rotary breakfast was in October at Bound Brook High School, and we purchased tickets for our children and grandchildren and for friends and their grandchildren. Sarah, Cortlandt and Kristen attended the breakfast with their parents. The Rotary members cooked and served breakfast to the guests while high school students, dressed up as Mickey and Minnie Mouse, gave balloons to the children. After they ate pancakes the grandchildren had a wonderful time racing up and down the corridors of the school. Mike did such a good job each year of arranging and carrying out the breakfasts that he received a Paul Harris Award from the Rotary Club for his efforts.

I decided that I needed exercise to keep fit when we were not in Rockport. Peter's family belonged to a YMCA in Flemington, so I decided to join also. I swam two or three times a week and felt much better for it. I usually swam in the evenings after work when the pool was not crowded. I was given several free guest tickets, so I took Janice and Kristen, and even Ralph Pritchard one time, as guests.

During the fall Kristen and I walked to downtown Clinton almost every weekend. Our favorite store was the Five and Ten Cent Store. We played hide and seek across the aisles and usually bought a little toy. We also visited the bookstore where I read books to Kristen at the little red tables. Clinton is a delightful town to visit. During the holidays they decorate the town and have special activities. For the Halloween season they put scarecrows on every corner and pumpkins on the doorsteps. The stores decorate their windows with witches, black cats, pumpkins and other seasonal figures. On Halloween weekend the town provides free rides for the children on fire engines. On Saturday of that weekend, as Kristen and I came to the bridge going into town, we saw a fire engine loading up with children. When we got nearer, the fire engine was full, but the driver invited Kristen and me to sit up front with him. He gave Kristen a rope to pull the bell so that it rang as we drove all over town. What an exciting day that was for both of us. At Christmas time there was always a big parade in Clinton with Santa on a fire engine. Kristen and her parents loved watching it.

December was full of the usual Christmas activities—a party at church, the Rotary dinner dance, the party at the Wagner College president's house, and a trip to see Rick's daughter, Julie, dance in the *Nutcracker.* All four children and their families came to Bound Brook for Christmas and we went to the Weber house for the Christmas night open house. On December 26 we opened gifts and enjoyed the family Christmas dinner. On the 27th we held an open house buffet for Cindy's friends from high school, and on the 31st we went out as always with Beverly and Dick Weber to welcome in the New Year.

We started 1998 with our winter vacation. We chose to go to Key West as Steve had told us great things about his experience there. We stayed at the Casa Marina Hotel in a room overlooking the ocean. We were on the first floor, just a step out the door and a run down the lawn to the ocean for a swim each day. There was coral at the water's edge so I had to walk out on a pier and dive in to avoid the sharp coral. We ate breakfast on our porch and, after my swim, walked all over town seeing the sights and trying different restaurants with dancing. We visited the Hemmingway house, the Little White House, President Truman's vacation retreat, and a beautiful old home, the Curray Mansion. At sundown we walked up to Old Mallory Square to watch various performers entertaining the tourists. There was a man who swallowed a sword, a trapeze artist, a juggler, a mime and other entertainers with groups of tourists circled about them. One day we rented a car and drove up the keys. We found a beautiful beach at Bahia Honda State Park and swam for over an hour. We went on to Marathon where we saw a movie, went out to dinner and ended a perfect day by dancing at a nightclub. We had such a good time that we persuaded the Deipnos to go with us to Key West the following year.

In March my Aunt Janet died and we drove to Winchester, Massachusetts for her funeral. Her daughter, Mimi, gave a beautiful eulogy for her mother. As part of the service Uncle Frank had asked the pianist to play their favorite dance tunes on a grand piano at the front of the church. Frank and Janet had always loved dancing together. Sometimes we saw them dancing on their porch at Rockport. The service was an emotional experience for me—Rockport wouldn't be the same without her. Our family enjoyed visiting her in the summer and she and Frank frequently joined us for picnics and dinners. After the service we talked to the Winchester relatives and noted that we wished we could get together next time for a happier occasion.

In April Peter and his family moved to a large house in Allentown, Pennsylvania as Pennick-Aramour had promoted

him to regional manager of eastern Pennsylvania. He and
Dorianne invited us to a picnic soon after they moved in. The
house had a huge living room, a playroom, dining room, office
and kitchen on the first floor. Sarah liked to dance in the living
room and leap off the coffee table to pirouette around the
spacious room. Next to the kitchen was a large fenced in porch
that was perfect for the children to play on. There were four
bedrooms on the second floor.

Every week in the spring Kristen and I walked through Clinton
to the playground a mile from her house. We stopped to watch
the geese and the ducks in the river; ran up and down the ramp
at a church on the way and played hide and seek behind the
church. When we reached the playground I pushed Kristen on
the swings and she played on the slides with the other children.
One day a man with three dogs came into the playground and
asked Kristen her name. Being shy she refused to answer, so
he called her "no name" each week when he saw her. After a
while Kristen gathered up her courage, went up to him and
said, "My name is Kristen." On our walk back to town, after we
had been in the playground, we stopped at the bakery for a
cookie, at the bookstore to browse and at the Five and Ten Cent
store to play hide and seek across the aisles. The sales lady was
fond of Kristen and always asked about her family. The last
stop on our weekly adventure was the ice cream store where I
bought a cone for each of us to eat on our way home.

We flew to Seattle to see Cindy, Denis and Thomas again in
May. On the first day of our visit we drove to Deception Pass
and had lunch in a quaint German restaurant in the tiny town of
Leavenworth. After lunch we visited an old mining town and
rode on the little train used for hauling ore from the mines. We
ate dinner in a rustic restaurant in town. The next day we took
Thomas to a Disney film about Camelot. The foliage in the
movie was such a bright green it did not look real. But then we
went for a hike in the Olympic Forest the next day and actually

saw moss just as green as that in the movie. We enjoyed Cindy's meals and on the last day we took them out for their favorite brunch, Eggs Benedict, and then to a restaurant beside the water for dinner. We enjoyed our nightly video watching with Cindy and Denis and, as always, the visit seemed much too short.

Cortlandt's second birthday party was held in Allentown, Pennsylvania on June 19th. The party was held on their big deck and the children played games and ate ice cream and cake. Cortlandt let go of his balloon and it went up in the air and became caught in a large tree. Steve had a tool that consisted of pliers on a long rod so he climbed up on the roof and retrieved the balloon much to the delight of all the guests. The next day we drove to Hempstead, Long Island to celebrate Mary's sixteenth birthday at a picnic in the back yard of the parsonage. Several days later we went to visit Steve's family and he announced that they were expecting a baby. We were thrilled and hugged Janice and Steve.

Mike and I attended a GBS seminar in Bar Harbor, Maine during the last week of June. We stayed in a lovely motel on a hill looking out on three small islands in the harbor. The first day we were there I decided to go swimming in the ocean while Mike was at a meeting. The water was cold, but I stayed in for my usual time of an hour. I was numb, but I didn't realize how cold the water was. When I came out of the water I was as close to hypothermia as I have ever been. I felt disoriented as I drove back to the motel and the hot shower that I took failed to warm me up. I climbed under the blankets in bed and decided that from then on I would swim in the outdoor pool at the motel. For the rest of the vacation I swam for an hour each day in the pool where I could enjoy looking at the harbor islands from a distance. We went kayaking on our last day and ate dinner in the elegant Bar Harbor Inn. We had crème brulee for dessert. Crème brulee on the menu is my way of identifying a first-class restaurant.

Our entire family gathered at Rockport for the first two weeks of July. We celebrated Kristen's birthday and watched the fourth of July parade and bonfire. During the last two weeks of July, Rick, Cathy and Beverly Weber were with me at Rockport and helped me proofread the annual Wagner College Bulletin. Cortlandt spent the first weekend in August at Rockport alone with Mike and me and we thoroughly enjoyed having him all to ourselves. He was fascinated with Thomas the Tank Engine and he spent most of his time pushing trains on every piece of furniture in the house. We took him to restaurants for dinner and he ran the trains on those tables too. He was a cheerful little fellow and loved to eat cereal. He would have been content to eat it for breakfast, lunch and dinner.

After Cortlandt left, Mike and I went to the GBS annual convention in Nashville, Tennessee. We stayed in the luxurious Opryland Hotel. The balcony of our room looked out over a lush conservatory of trees and waterfalls that were inside the gigantic glass dome of the hotel. While Mike attended meetings I read Katherine Graham's autobiography on our balcony. We ate in several restaurants within the hotel complex and spent one evening at the Grand Ole Opry. Another night we rode up the river on a majestic paddle wheeler, The General Jackson. We danced to banjo music on the deck and ate dinner while watching the sunset over the water. We visited the capitol and the Hermitage, Andrew Jackson's home, and attended a country music church service on Sunday. My favorite entertainment was a concert of Patsy Cline's music sung by a woman with a voice nearly identical to Patsy Cline's. On our last night in Nashville, GBS treated all the franchisees and their spouses to dinner and dancing at a fancy country club. We really enjoyed our week in Nashville. Over the years that Mike operated his franchise, the GBS conventions gave us the opportunity to enjoy a number of charming cities that we otherwise would never have visited such as San Diego, Colorado Springs, Cancun, Las Vegas and Nashville.

We celebrated Mike's and Sarah's birthdays in Rockport after we came back from Nashville. On Labor Day weekend the whole family joined us again at Rockport. We had another fun filled weekend with games, picnics and much reminiscing. I went back to work at Wagner in September and the first week I was there I received a phone call from Steve who had just learned the results of Janice's amniocentesis. He said, "Guess what the test showed about the baby." I said, "It's a boy?" He replied, "No, guess again." So, I said, "It's a girl?" He again replied, "No." I was dumbfounded. Then he laughed excitedly and said, "It's two girls—twins." I was so excited that I yelled to the whole registrar's office, "Steve and Janice are having twins!"

Sarah and Cortlandt spent the weekend of October 24th with us in Bound Brook. We took them to a pumpkin farm and each of them chose a pumpkin that we took back to our house and carved faces in. Steve and Janice invited us over to their house for dinner and Cortlandt and Sarah enjoyed playing with Kristen. On Sunday they dressed up in their fancy clothes and joined us at church. That afternoon we drove them back home and took their family out to dinner at Friendly's restaurant.

Kristen and I continued our walks during the fall. One Saturday while we were at the Clinton playground we saw some hot air balloons above us. We followed them to a field in back of the playground. Kristen saw a balloon far off in the distance that looked like a speck to me. She told me that it was the pumpkin balloon, and sure enough, when it came closer it had the face of a pumpkin on it. We were both very excited to see so many colorful balloons. While Kristen played on the slide at the playground I talked to some of the mothers there. They told me of other playgrounds that their children enjoyed. Kristen and I later visited the Annandale and the White Oak playgrounds that the ladies suggested and Kristen really liked the latter.

In mid-November Peter received an offer to become the head wrestling coach at Franklin and Marshall College. He was overjoyed and accepted with alacrity even though this would necessitate another move for his family, from Allentown to Lancaster, Pennsylvania. Peter had entered the business world when he could not find a suitable wrestling coaching job, but his heart remained in the world of wrestling. He worked hard in his position at Pennick-Aramour and strove to be a good manager for the company, but his new job at Franklin and Marshall brought out the zest and enthusiasm that he had not felt since he left the Naval Academy. He and Dorianne found a charming home in Lancaster, in a friendly neighborhood full of children. The elementary school was within walking distance in a residential area with little traffic.

To ease the stress on Dorianne, Mike and I offered to treat the family to a brief vacation at a farm near Lancaster before the move took place. On October 28 they visited a working Amish farm in the area and stayed in a quaint cottage. Sarah and Cortland enjoyed climbing the ladder to their beds in the loft. They rode on farm equipment modeled for children and played in a large playhouse during the day. They ate big country meals and enjoyed a relaxed two days before the work of moving started. After they moved into their new house, Dorianne invited the family to Peter's birthday party. We met the neighbors and Peter's colleagues from the college and everyone seemed friendly and interesting.

Early in December the Twin Boros Scholarship Foundation honored Mike as their Man of the Year. They hosted a nice dinner in a Bound Brook restaurant and the children and grandchildren, as well as many friends, were there to see him honored. The Twin Boros Foundation raises money to give four scholarships annually to qualified high school seniors from Bound Brook and South Bound Brook. The foundation was started in 1984 by an eighty-year-old man from our church,

Hugo Kladivko, who suggested that if everyone in town gave a penny a day we could collect enough money to give scholarships. He discussed his idea with Mike and together they persuaded several leading citizens to help organize the endeavor. Mike accepted the job of secretary of the foundation and has served in that position ever since. Over the years a great deal of money has been collected and many scholarships have been awarded.

At Christmas time we flew to Seattle for our early celebration with the Lavoies. We spent another marvelous week with them and one of the most interesting trips we took was to Mount Saint Helen. We saw an Imax movie depicting the eruption of the volcano that blew off the top of the mountain. It was terrifying to witness and Thomas kept saying, "The mountain fell down," over and over again. When we drove up the side of the mountain it was black and bare with trees that looked like matchsticks strewn over the ground. During our visit we bought and decorated a Christmas tree with the family and shared our gifts together. Cindy and Denis' gift to us was a cruise from Istanbul to Athens in June for our 45th anniversary. We were completely surprised and thrilled with such a generous gift.

When we returned home we went to see Julie in the *Nutcracker* and took Mary, Julie, Rick and Cathy to dinner afterwards. We celebrated Christmas with the rest of the family on December 26th. As always we ended the year by celebrating New Years Eve with Beverly and Dick Weber. We went to a German club in Plainfield, New Jersey, where we danced to Viennese waltzes all evening and enjoyed a typical German dinner after the New Year came in.

I had decided that I would give a baby shower for Janice in January. I had sent out invitations in November and told everyone it was to be a surprise. We decorated the house with balloons and prepared a big buffet. Everyone brought two gifts for the twins and many of them were extremely generous. Millie Sheehan and Beverly Weber each brought a high chair and Janice's brother, John, brought a double stroller. The gifts took up one corner of our living room. Janice thought that she was coming to dinner at our house and when she came in the front door and saw the crowd awaiting her she was stunned. Her mother had given her a shower for Kristen so she never expected a shower for a subsequent baby. The grandchildren enjoyed sampling the refreshments and watching Janice open the gifts. Beverly brought a number of delicious desserts, much to everyone's delight. After the shower Janice was well supplied with clothes and equipment for the two new babies.

Steve bought a house in Whitehouse Station at a bargain price. He planned to fix it up and sell it. The house had a large yard with big trees. As the house was being renovated, Janice began to think it would be a good house to live in for a family with three little children. The house in Clinton was on the main street with very little play area for children. So they decided to rent out the two apartments in the Clinton house and move to Whitehouse Station. Steve had done a marvelous job fixing up the house in Whitehouse Station. He refinished the kitchen and big bathroom on the first floor and bought all new appliances. They moved in on January 30th, just two weeks before the twins were born. They couldn't get their queen-size bed up the stairs, so we bought them a king-size bed that folded in half and could be brought up the stairs. They gave us their queen-size bed for the guestroom at our house. The king-size bed came in handy as all five of them frequently slept in that bed.

17

More Grandchildren

Nicole and Victoria Schuyler were born on February 17, 1999. Nicole came into the world five minutes before Victoria and they were both adorable. The hospital allowed Janice to stay in her room for a few extra days until the twins were ready to come home. Janice got very little sleep those first few months. The twins ate every two hours and no sooner would one finish the bottle, but the second one was ready to eat. They were so small that each one took a long time to finish her bottle so there was very little time for Janice to rest between feedings. I decided that I would take Fridays off to help her and even another day some weeks. I worked Saturdays and some Sundays at Wagner to make up the time. Steve was home on weekends to give her some relief. I tried to let her sleep when I was there. She was exhausted, but she kept going and napped when she could.

Janice was so proud and thrilled with the twins that she had a professional photographer take their picture when they were two months old. Victoria had thick black hair and Nicole had none. From the beginning they had two very distinct personalities. They were just beautiful and wonderful to be with. I continued to take Kristen for walks and Mike and I spent numerous evenings with the family.

Cindy and Denis had been trying to have another baby for several years. After a number of failed attempts to become pregnant by artificial means, they decided to adopt a baby. The adoption agency required them to undergo almost a year of preparation. They had to provide references about their character and take classes on adopting a child. Their vitae were given to parents who wished to have their babies adopted. The biological parents who approved of Cindy and Denis as adoptive parents indicated their approval to the agency and then Cindy and Denis could select the family that they wished to adopt from. After they made their choice they visited with the expectant parents and each couple was pleased with the other. The expectant parents were mainly concerned that their baby live in a loving family.

The expectant mother lived in Las Vegas and when she went into labor she called Cindy and Denis who flew there immediately and were able to be in the delivery room when the baby was born. As soon as he was born the doctor handed him to Cindy. He was a beautiful boy and Cindy and Denis named him Lucas. Cindy, Denis, Thomas and Lucas stayed in a motel for about a week until all the papers were signed making Lucas legally theirs. During that week they got to know the birth parents and both couples liked the other.

When we made our semi-annual trip to Seattle on Memorial Day weekend we met and cuddled Lucas. He was an adorable little baby boy with blonde hair and blue eyes. Lucas was christened during our visit and we met many of Denis and Cindy's friends at the reception afterwards. We enjoyed going on a trip around the harbor with the family. The guide on the boat told us of the many activities in the harbor. The tour ended with a trip through the Chittenden Locks. It was very interesting to see how the locks filled and emptied.

When we returned to Bound Brook we prepared for our cruise through the Greek Isles. On June 4th Cathy drove us to JFK

Airport and we flew to Frankfurt, arriving at six in the morning.
I sat in a daze for several hours at the airport waiting for the
next leg of our flight. I finally dosed off for a short while after
we boarded our plane to Istanbul. In Istanbul we rode in a bus
for almost an hour and finally arrived at the Hilton Hotel on a
hill overlooking the Bosphorus. Our room was luxurious with
a magnificent view. We went right to bed and slept for a few
hours. When we awoke Mike took a shower and I went for a
nice long swim in the large pool at the hotel. That night we
went on a tour to see the fabled whirling dervishes. Afterward
we had a multi-course repast of Turkish delicacies in the great
hall of the building. We spent two days in Istanbul and loved
every minute of it. We visited the Blue Mosque and the Saint
Sophia Mosque the first morning and ate lunch at an outdoor
café. In the afternoon we toured the ornate Topkapi Palace and
stopped at a charming little hotel to rest afterwards over coffee
and ice cream. Then we bought many souvenir gifts for the
Deipnos and other friends. With our usual lack of common
sense, we bought heavy tile gifts to lug home in our suitcases.
We came back to the Hilton for a swim and a rest and that
evening we walked to a romantic restaurant with vines and
twinkling lights overhead.

The next morning at breakfast on the hotel veranda overlooking
the sea, we decided to explore the market place. I was so worried
that someone would steal Mike's wallet that I walked right behind
him. That annoyed him, so I finally stopped and walked along
side of him. We left the market after purchasing a small figurine
of a whirling dervish and walked a considerable distance to
see the Suleyman Mosque. On the way we walked through a
college and then explored a small mosque that we discovered.
All the mosques that we saw were awesome, especially the
Suleyman, which was gigantic. We walked by an ancient
viaduct on the way back to the hotel and had lunch in a small
Turkish restaurant along the main avenue. Then we checked
out of our room and took a taxi to our cruise ship. Denis had

upgraded our cruise tickets and we were thrilled with the luxurious suite we found ourselves in after boarding the ship. Our room had a full size balcony with glass doors leading out to it. We could sit and watch the sunset and have magnificent views of all the places where we stopped.

As we sailed through the Dardanelles I imagined Jason and Medea fleeing through them with the Golden Fleece and Medea's father, King Aetes, in hot pursuit. Euripides' play, *Medea,* was the first reading in MDS 101 for all freshmen in Wagner College, so I had read it over and over again and enjoyed reliving it on our trip. The food on the ship was delicious and we had five restaurants to choose from. We danced in the Starlight Room after dinner each night.

We slept well that first night and when we opened the curtains on the glass door in the morning we were staring at Mt. Athos. We sat on the balcony as we moved by it and then went to breakfast. The first stop of the cruise was Kusadasi, a seaside resort on the Aegean Sea. As we explored the open market for toys for the grandchildren, I noticed that my old leather eyeglasses case in Mike's back pocket was gone. Someone had taken it, probably thinking it was a wallet. While we were discussing it a lady came over to us and told us she would give us another case. She took us to her husband's store and gave me a nice new case. We thanked her and talked to her for a while. She was a Dutch woman who had married a Turkish man and they were trying to eke out a living with their little eyeglass store. As we continued through the market, past several rug stores, Mike was tempted to buy an Oriental carpet but I talked him out of it.

We took a bus to Ephesus, an amazingly well preserved ancient Greek city in Turkey. As we rounded a curve on the way we looked back at the town of Kusadasi with its beautiful harbor in the Aegean Sea. We explored Ephesus for quite some time and saw the vestiges of its original library, the Temple of Hadrian, the Baths of Scholastica and the public latrines. On the outskirts of town there was a gigantic amphitheater, the Theatre of Ephesus. This was the most spectacular building of the city and remained nearly intact. The bus also took us to see the Church of Saint John. At the end of the day we returned to the ship for dinner, dancing and a night's rest.

The next cruise stop was Rhodes, an old walled city that is very popular with tourists. Over the centuries it has been occupied by many civilizations—Greek, Roman, Byzantine, Christian and Turkish. It has beautiful beaches as well as magnificent man-made structures. It has been called the most lustrous pearl of the Mediterranean. Mike and I went to the beach on our first morning there and saw women in topless bathing suits lying on the beach. I left Mike "reading" on the beach while I went swimming. We went back to the ship to change and eat lunch and then we took a taxi to Lindos about an hour's drive down the coast from Rhodes. At Lindos there is an acropolis high on a cliff overlooking the sea. The climb to the peak is treacherous. We climbed up steep narrow stairs along the side of the cliff with one side exposed to a sheer drop straight down. The view from the top was spectacular, looking down at harbors on either side of the enormous crag. When we returned to Rhodes we visited the old town inside the walls of the city. We dined and danced again that night and, as we were sleeping, the ship sailed on to our next destination.

We awoke the next morning to a magnificent view of Santorini, our favorite location of the whole trip. The island of Santorini has a history of violent volcanic eruptions over the last 3500 years. What is left today is half a crater with rugged volcanic cliffs rising out of the water on one side and natural slopes and beaches on the other side. Fira is the capital and Athinos is the port city. Cruise ships land on the cliff side and tourists must take a cable car up to top to visit Fira with its sparkling white houses and churches looking down on the royal blue sea of the crater. The churches have round blue domes that match the color of the sea and little white crosses sitting on top of the domes. The town of Fira is immaculate with narrow streets winding between its buildings. After a bit of shopping in Fira we took a taxi to Kamari, a beach on the other side of the island. I swam back and forth between two cliffs while Mike "read" in the midst of topless sunbathers. We rode back to Fira for lunch and took many pictures before returning to our ship.

The last stop on our cruise was Athens. We had a huge suite at a first class hotel, thanks to Denis' upgrading of our tickets. We toured Athens on our last two days and found it inspiring. When we arrived in our hotel we called two Greek nursing friends, Vassiliki Lanara and Aphrodite Reyes, who were my fellow students at Columbia University Graduate School. I had written to them that we were coming to Athens and when I called they were delighted to hear my voice. They insisted on picking us up at our hotel and taking us out to lunch. We met them in the lobby and they took us to a charming restaurant. Vassiliki ordered for us as the menu was in Greek. We had a good time reminiscing about old times. After lunch they hailed a taxi for us and we went off to the Acropolis.

At the Acropolis we climbed the hill to inspect the famous monuments. We saw the Temple of Athena Niki, the Erechtheion with the porch of the Caryatides, the Theater of Dionysus and the Parthenon. We could imagine the grandeur of Athens from seeing these beautiful structures. I was especially interested in the Theater of Dionysus as we had studied Dionysus in one of the IDS courses at Wagner College.

We left the Acropolis and took a taxi to the market place and relaxed over coffee at a small bistro. After exploring a few stores we had dinner at the Poseidon, an outdoor café in the historic square of the old city of Athens. Our table was under vine covered trellises and we enjoyed the enchanting atmosphere as we ate our delicious Greek meal. After dinner we took a taxi back to our hotel and collapsed into bed.

The next day the hotel provided us with a complimentary breakfast and then we took a taxi back to the market place. We passed the changing of the guard at the palace on the way and saw the Greek guards in their colorful uniforms. We spent the day in the market looking at the colorful shops and buying more gifts and souvenirs. To finish the day we celebrated our anniversary at Milton's Restaurant and Piano Bar at the entrance to the market. The dinner was fantastic, ending with crème brulee and another divine cream dessert. We swapped our desserts back and forth trying to decide which was more delicious. On our walk back to the hotel after dinner we ran into a rousing political demonstration. Circumventing the crowd, we continued our starlight stroll. The next morning we bordered the plane for home. What a marvelous treat we had to celebrate our forty-five years of marriage.

Cathy met us in New York and told us the wonderful news that she was pregnant. We were so happy for her and Rick. Soon after our return we went to Rockport with Steve's and Peter's families. We celebrated Cortlandt's second birthday at the Rockport house with thirty of his relatives. Jim Tarpy, his uncle, had made a large table with a track layout for Thomas the Tank Engine, including bridges, stations, cranes and an assortment of engines and cars that were part of the Thomas the Tank Engine ensemble. It was a magnificent gift and Cortlandt adored it. Cortlandt's fascination with Thomas the Tank Engine continued through the end of the year. Peter made him a Thomas the Tank Engine costume out of a cardboard box for Halloween, which pleased him greatly.

At the end of June we went to Rockville, Maryland for the Bar Mitzvah of our nephew, Michael. At the ceremony in the synagogue Michael presented an excellent talk with a smattering of dry humor. The rabbi told the audience how much he enjoyed having Michael for a student. After the ceremony there was a reception in the social hall of the synagogue. That evening Steve and Carol hosted a big celebration for Michael in the Rockville Community Center. A DJ played young people's music and Sarah, Kristen and Cortlandt enjoyed the dancing as much as Michael and his friends. Nicole and Victoria sat in their seats on the table and didn't seem to mind the loud music at all. The DJ also played a few numbers the adults could dance to, which we appreciated. There were prizes and favors for the children and everyone had a great time. The next morning the relatives gathered at Big Boy's for brunch before we left for home.

About this time our small car, a 1995 Ford Aspire that I used to commute to Wagner College, started misbehaving. We had spent over $3000 on repairs and it still didn't work. We looked at a number of new cars for me to travel back and forth to work. Then we saw a bright yellow Volkswagen bug and I fell in love with it. Mike and I splurged and bought the car of my dreams. We registered it in my name, my first ownership of a car. Everyone who saw it liked it and said how cute it was. Of all the cars I had ever driven this was my favorite. I received a number of yellow toy VW bugs from friends and relatives. I placed them on top of the hutch cabinet in the kitchen and none of the grandchildren were allowed to play with them.

We drove my new car to Rockport to be with the family on the fourth of July. Dorianne brought tee shirts with American flags on the front for all the grandchildren. At the holiday parade we took pictures of the children in their shirts including Lucas, Nicole and Victoria in their baby seats. The older children were waving flags and it was very festive and patriotic. There was no problem identifying the Schuyler clan at the parade. Cathy, Rick, Mary, Julie and a friend came up on the fifth. Julie and her friend each took over the care of one of the twins and Janice enjoyed the freedom this provided.

Later that month, Rick was transferred from his church in Hempstead, Long Island to the United Methodist Church of Danbury, Connecticut. He had asked for the transfer in order to be closer to Mary and Julie. Their new home was a large white colonial with nine rooms, a garage and a screened-in porch across the back of the house. Mary and Julie each had her own bedroom. Julie chose purple and yellow, her favorite colors, to decorate her room. The new house was in a lovely residential section of Danbury with many trees and a pond nearby. Shortly after that we learned that Cindy and Denis had moved into a bigger house in Seattle, with a magnificent view of Puget Sound and the Olympic Mountains.

Beverly Weber and Millie Sheehan spent a week with me at Rockport in the middle of July, and during the first two weeks of August we entertained my brother David and his wife, Mary, as well as Steve's and Peter's families. I gave a big birthday party for Mike and David on August 7th with thirty-five guests, and the next day we had a party for Sarah's birthday with thirty-four guests. The good times were rolling.

We returned to Bound Brook for a short time and took care of Cortlandt and Sarah for a weekend, then returned to Rockport for Labor Day weekend. It was quieter than usual for that holiday as we were alone with Steve's family, but, as always, we had a great time with them. Steve's family slept in the dormitory room, the biggest room in the house, as he and Janice had the largest number of children. Victoria and Nicole slept in their little seats on the floor of the dormitory room and the rest of their family slept in beds. Every morning when I came downstairs the twins would be sitting in their seats on the floor of the dining room smiling up at me. What a great way to start the day!

Mike and I drove to Rockport every weekend in September, going to the movies and dancing on Saturday nights while we were there. At the end of the month we attended the fiftieth reunion of my class at Winchester High School. I was nervous when I arrived, fearing that I wouldn't know anyone. I asked Mike to stay close to me so I wouldn't feel isolated. As I walked into the lobby of the hotel a loud voice rang out, "Connie Smith!" It was Bobby Horn, the president of the alumni class of 1949. He and I had been schoolmates from kindergarten to high school and he was very jovial. Many of my classmates remembered me because of my fuzzy hair. Soon Mike came up to me and announced that he had found my best friend from Winchester, Ruthie Sheehan. She was just as nice as I remembered her and we sat with her and her husband at dinner. I had a wonderful time talking with them and dancing with Mike to a band composed of my classmates. They played the music of the forties and we loved dancing to it. Bobby Horn was the master of ceremonies and reminded us of the antics of our classmates when we were in high school. We sang old songs of the forties together and everyone knew the words. A photo was taken of the whole class, which I treasure. I was so glad that we had decided to go to the reunion.

In the fall I continued to take Kristen on weekends. We could no longer walk to the Clinton Park after she moved to Whitehouse Station, but we drove to different parks. There was a cute little park near her new home called Pickle Park. We played hide and seek, threw tennis balls into the basketball hoops, and played on the swings and slides. A path wound through the park with various pieces of exercise equipment along the way. She liked to try the chin-ups, push ups and other exercises as we progressed around the park. Sometimes we drove back to Clinton to take our old walk there. Kristen also enjoyed coming to our house to play with the toys we kept on hand for the grandchildren.

Victoria and Nicole spent most of their time in the living room of their house. They sat in their seats and played with toys or watched television. When they were eight months old they showed interest in learning to crawl. One day one of them actually started to crawl. The other one spent all her time rocking back and forth on her hands and knees even when she was in her crib. By the next day she too could crawl. Competition between them began early. A few months later when they were ready to walk they both took off together from one side of the living room and walked across the room.

Mike and I attended a GBS convention in Florida in November. We stayed at an elegant resort on Amelia Island in a room that looked out at the ocean. I swam twice a day and on the last day someone on the elevator told me that swimming was not allowed if there was a red flag on the beach. He said that the red flag had been up all week. I had never seen or heard of the flag, but I did swim in the hotel pool on our last day. We danced in the lobby during the cocktail hour and dined on delicious food at the hotel. We bought an apple and a muffin each evening at the deli and ate breakfast on our balcony looking out to sea. One afternoon while we were there, we took a bus into the town of Fernandina Beach to buy some Christmas gifts. We discovered a number of magnificent Victorian houses in the town. We found out that a Schuyler relative had designed several of the houses and a lovely old church, so we took pictures of many of the old homes.

For Thanksgiving we flew to Seattle and visited Cindy and Denis' new home. It was lovely, built in the sixties with spacious rooms, polished oak floors and magnificent views. Every room except the kitchen had huge picture windows overlooking the sound and the mountains. There was a formal living room and dining room, a large den and an ample kitchen on the first floor. On the lower level there was a big finished playroom, a computer room and a private guestroom and bath behind the playroom. Each of the three bedrooms on the second floor had a panoramic view. It was a dream house for them. Thomas had joined a T-Ball team and was a good little hitter. We went to see one of his games and he ran like the wind for such a little four-year-old. We also visited Sarah Perkins and her family again. Her children enjoyed playing with Thomas and shared all their toys with him. We enjoyed talking to Sarah and Scott over dinner.

Early in December we were invited to Shirley and Ed Saxby's fiftieth wedding anniversary in South Carolina. On the spur of the moment we decided to join them and flew down for the celebration. The party was in the home of their son Hal, and it was great to see our nieces and nephews on Mike's side of the family. They were stunned and delighted to see us and we all enjoyed ourselves immensely. An army chaplain led Shirley and Ed in the renewal of their vows and the ceremony was followed by a nice reception in Hal and Tracy's house.

Cindy and Denis came east with the boys for Christmas and we had a marvelous family reunion at our house. On the 27th Beverly Weber gave a baby shower for Cathy and all of our immediate family were there, as well as my brother Steve, his wife, Carol, and their son Jordon. The Deipnos were there, as were old friends Mary Parenteau, Shelia Fuhrman and Mitey Weber. Beverly prepared her usual elegant dinner and the guests were seated at formally set tables in the living and dining rooms. After a delicious dessert our grandchildren had a great time playing with the toys of Beverly's grandchildren and hiding in the playroom closet.

The new century began on a sad note. My Uncle Frank died. Now my aunts and uncles from the other two houses at Rockport were gone. We had always looked forward to visiting Frank and Janet and having them come to parties with our family. Frank had a wonderful sense of humor and was always jolly and fun to be with. The grandchildren loved to visit Aunt Janet and Uncle Frank at their house and play with their marble game. They also enjoyed going down to visit Aunt Marion and Uncle Jay when they were alive. I felt very close to my aunts and uncles at Rockport. Frank and Janet's only child, Mimi, inherited her parents' house and she and her husband, Joe Delehant, were most gracious to our grandchildren as they continued to visit their house. Mimi and Joe came to our family picnics and dinners, so the family tie remains. We picked up Cathy in Danbury on our way to Frank's funeral in Winchester. We ate lunch at my Uncle Bob's house before the service. Mimi gave a lovely eulogy for her father at the service and our Cathy also paid him a warm tribute. We stopped at Cathy and Rick's house for dinner on the way home.

The big event in February was the birth of Cathy and Rick's baby. On February 28th just before midnight, Cathy delivered a beautiful little girl. She just missed having her birthday on February 29th. Rick and Cathy named her Charis Van Rensselaer Edwards, with the nickname of Carrie. She weighed nine and a half pounds and Cathy had to have a Caesarian section to bring her into the world. We drove up to see her the next day and she was gorgeous! We held her and rocked her and felt very fortunate to have another wonderful grandchild. We also celebrated the first birthday of Victoria and Nicole in February. They were given two parties, one at their house and one at ours. There was an abundance of gifts and great excitement with balloons, favors, two cakes and ice cream.

A third memorable event in February 2000 was Beverly and Dick Weber's fiftieth wedding anniversary. We gave them a party at Patullo's restaurant to celebrate the occasion. A buffet dinner was provided and the guests told anecdotes about them and toasted their happiness. A band played music for dancing and Beverly and Dick seemed pleased and happy. We had known the Webers nearly all of their married life and felt very close to them.

In March we visited Carrie again and she was even prettier. Cathy was nursing her and she was a happy baby. Her two older sisters, Mary and Julie, were delighted with her. We went to see Mary in her school play at the end of March. For Easter we visited Peter's family in Lancaster and after church we took them out to the Cracker Barrel Restaurant for Easter dinner. They enjoyed playing checkers at the restaurant while we waited for our table.

During the spring semester Kristen spent almost every Saturday with me. She liked to play with our small plastic Disney figurines of princes and princesses. She made castles of Lego for them to live in or lined them up in long parades around the kitchen floor. She and I enjoyed making cookies together for her family. She also liked to draw pictures and color. When we were going to have company for dinner she would set the dining room table, make place cards and even help me dust. In the cold weather we sometimes went to the Disney Store in the mall or if it was a nice day we went to the park for a while.

On May 5th Cathy called me at work and asked if she could come down to Wagner and take me out to lunch for my birthday. She arrived at noon carrying Carrie in a bright green sling that looked like a pea pod. She was adorable cuddled up in that sling and I proudly took Cathy around and introduced her and Carrie to everyone in the registrar's office. We ended up eating in the cafeteria as it was much easier than driving to a restaurant. Of course I enjoyed introducing them to my faculty friends and fellow administrators at lunch. I told Cathy how much I appreciated her wonderful birthday surprise.

Our annual Mother's Day and birthday celebration at Patullo's was a success as usual. Ten days later we attended Carrie's christening at Rick's church and the reception at her house. Kristen came with us and she enjoyed seeing the christening and playing at the house afterwards. A week later we returned to Cathy and Rick's house for dinner on our way to Rockport with Steve's family to open the house for the season. We opened the house, turned on the water and vacuumed the rooms. We took the children to Bearskin Neck for candy and they were happy. We left at the end of the weekend as we all had to go back to work. On June 8th we had a party for Steve's birthday at our Bound Brook house and then drove to Rockport the next day with Peter and his family for a few days.

After we returned to Bound Brook Steve invited us to dinner at his house. When we arrived at his house late in the afternoon, Steve looked at us and told us that they were going to have another baby. I was so excited that I grabbed Janice and hugged her and then threw my arms around Steve and we both began to cry for joy. They soon found out that the baby was a boy and they were even more excited. The baby would be just two years younger than the twins.

We returned to Rockport the next weekend for a summer filled with parties, picnics, dinners and fun. The entire family was there for the fourth of July and Kristen celebrated her birthday the following day. One of Mike's projects that summer was to refinish the downstairs bedroom and make it into a playroom. He removed the large old painted bureau and the big double bed from the room and replaced them with a hide-a-bed couch, greatly enlarging the play area, while still retaining the room as a bedroom when needed. We put a thick new rug on the floor and moved a TV set into the room, a welcome renovation. The children loved watching *Tom and Jerry Cartoons* when it rained or while the adults talked and played games in the dining room.

Over Labor Day weekend, we had a big picnic with all of our family plus the Gordons and Mimi and Joe. Mary and David's daughter Marion and her son, Sage, came for the first time. Sage was a cute little fellow, the same age as Nicole and Victoria, and he enjoyed playing with his cousins. The adults played *Trivial Pursuit* and other games, which David enjoyed as he is very competitive and always likes the challenge of games. While we played *Trivial Pursuit* Victoria sat in the middle of the table; later we had to put her on the floor because she spilled all the game cards out of the box. It didn't bother me, as the grandchildren can do no wrong in my mind, and the other guests seemed to take it in their stride.

In the fall Kristen and Steve helped us clean out our garage in Bound Brook. Steve had offered to convert one-half of our two-car-garage into an office for use in our retirement. The garage had never had a car in it, but it had accumulated piles of junk over the years. Amazingly we cleaned it out in one day. The biggest problem was getting rid of our camping trailer, which had not been used for thirty years. It was in excellent shape, with sleeping room for four, a table and benches, plus a screened addition on the outside. We finally found a retired couple in our church who were campers, and we gave it to them, much to their delight. Steve built us an attractive office with carpeting and plentiful recessed lighting in the ceiling. I suggested that he build a bay window at the far end of the office to let the sun shine in and give us fresh air, which he did. We were thrilled with our new office and, as soon as Mike retired, we moved the furniture from his old office into it. We decorated it with pictures of Rockport and it became our favorite room. It is bright and cheerful and we spend a great deal of time in it together working on our various projects.

In October we visited Tom and Simi Long in Atlanta. Bruce McCreary, Beverly Weber, Mike and I flew down and they met us at the airport. They were most gracious to us and we spent a delightful weekend together. We discussed *Gone with the Wind* on Saturday night, just like old times when the Longs regularly attended the Deipno meetings. On Sunday we joined the Longs at their church and attended Simi's adult Bible class. We concluded the weekend with a gourmet dinner cooked by Simi. We enjoyed seeing the Long children again at dinner.

During the last week in October Mike and I took a four-day vacation in Myrtle Beach, South Carolina. The ocean was warm and I swam every day. Our room had a lovely view of the ocean, as did the motel dining room. A charming waiter treated us royally and the food was first-rate. We walked to a theater on two of the evenings to see recent movies and, on the third evening, we went to the Sea Captain's House, a charming restaurant on the beach. On our last day we rented a car and visited Brookgreen Gardens. These gardens, offering the finest collection of outdoor American sculpture, are on four former plantations amidst giant moss-draped oaks and magnificent gardens and fountains. With over 150 sculptures to see it took us half a day to go through the gardens. It was a marvelous experience.

We returned home in time for Halloween. Kristen and Sarah both wore Snow White costumes, Thomas was Spiderman, Lucas was a pumpkin and Carrie was an angel. Cortlandt was the Titanic, as he had developed a new special interest in the doomed ship. He had read about it in many books and knew all the statistics about the crew and the passengers. He asked his father to make him a Halloween costume of the Titanic. Peter took a big cardboard carton and made a stunning model of the ship. It fit over Cortlandt's head so it surrounded his waist and his arms came out of the portholes. Cortlandt led the parade at school and won first prize for his costume.

In December we joined the Lavoies again for an early Christmas. Thomas was six years old and Lucas was one and a half. We bought a tree and trimmed it together and then went shopping at Sears. Thomas found an outfit that he wanted to buy for Lucas. After Lucas opened it he put it on and gave Thomas a big hug. While we were there, Thomas played games on the computer while Lucas repeatedly watched a video of classical music for babies. One of the pictures on the video was a colorful castle with balls on top of its turrets. The video showed a child hammering the balls with a plastic hammer in time with the music. Lucas loved this sequence on the video and asked Santa for that castle. Santa came early to Seattle that year and left the castle for Lucas. When Lucas saw it he was ecstatic. After a wonderful five days with the Lavoies we returned to Bound Brook and celebrated Christmas with the rest of the family on the 26th.

18

And More Grandchildren

The year 2001 began with a big snowstorm. Kristen and I built a large snow girl in our yard. Kristen came to our house every Saturday in January and we ate dinner at her house frequently. Janice hosted a birthday party for Victoria and Nicole on February 17th even though her delivery date was only a week away. Pete and Cathy came to the party with their families and the children played games and ate ice cream and cake.

On February 24th Bradford John Schuyler was born. Mike and I stayed with the girls at their house for three days and nights while Janice, Steve and Brad stayed in the hospital. Victoria was the only one who would sleep in her own bed. She was always very excited when I came to get her up in the morning. Kristen and Nicole slept on the two couches in the living room where they were accustomed to sleeping. I brought our own sheets and Mike and I slept in Janice and Steve's bed. We took the girls to visit their parents and Brad each day. Rick, Cathy and Carrie also came down for a visit. We ordered a pizza for all of us the evening that they came. Taking care of the girls was such fun for us and they apparently enjoyed it also, as Kristen asked her mother when she was going to have another baby so Nana and Grandpa could stay with them again. Brad was a contented baby from the very beginning. He seemed to have a gentle nature. Janice and Steve were thrilled with their adorable baby boy. After he came home Janice held him a great deal of the time and when she needed both hands she put him in his little seat on the kitchen floor near her.

At the beginning of March we took Kristen with us to Danbury to celebrate Carrie's first birthday. Carrie looked adorable in her bright red velvet dress and she had a great time ripping the paper off her gifts. Some friends of Rick and Cathy were there with their children and Cathy had a full schedule of planned activities to keep the children entertained. Cathy had made a delicious dinner and Carrie enjoyed blowing out the candles on her big homemade cake.

Peter and his family came to see Brad when he was a few weeks old; then we went down to Lancaster to spend the next weekend with them. I bought new outfits for all the grandchildren for Easter including twin dresses for Sarah and Kristen. On Easter we drove to Danbury and spent the holiday with Rick, Cathy and Carrie. Carrie looked adorable in her new Easter dress and we all went out for Easter dinner after church. We were impressed with how precocious Carrie was. She walked at ten months and at thirteen months she knew her letters, could say a number of words and sing numerous tunes of hymns. She was a jolly bouncy child, but also loved to sit in our laps and be read to. She liked to talk on the phone, play with her sister Julie and go to the mall to ride on the carousel. It was always a joy to visit her and her parents.

In April Mike brought Kristen to Wagner College to have lunch with me. I enjoyed introducing her to my friends in the cafeteria and to all the ladies in the registrar's office after lunch. Then I went back to work while Mike took Kristen to visit the Staten Island Zoo. They picked me up at work at the end of the day and Mike and Kristen followed me home. Kristen and Carrie were the only grandchildren to visit my office at Wagner.

Early in May Steve and Janice invited us to their house for my birthday and later we took Janice out to dinner for her birthday. Then on Mother's Day we had our annual celebration of both birthdays and Mother's Day. Herbie Patullo had retired and sold his restaurant, but he recommended Ellery's, a restaurant owned by his nephew in the next town. We reserved the second floor for our family party. There was a long table in the middle of the room for dinner and several side tables along the wall for the children to play games on and pile the gifts on. I brought favors of balls, paints and paint books and other activities to entertain the children. Their favorite activities were crawling under the tables, running up and down the room and throwing balls to each other. We had to keep a close eye on the twins to see that they did not fall down the stairs, but they seemed to be well diverted with all the toys to play with. We had the whole menu to choose from so everyone was satisfied with a delicious dinner of his or her own choice. Mike bought corsages for all the mothers and there were lots of gifts for mothers and birthday celebrants. We all had a great time at the party and decided to continue the celebration as an annual event at the new location.

In June we gave a birthday party for Steve on the deck that Steve had built on our Bound Brook house years earlier. Peter and Cathy came with their families and we all had fun. We opened Rockport for the summer at the end of the month, but returned to New Jersey shortly after that to meet our new grandchild, Malcolm Thayer Schuyler, who was born on July 1st in Lancaster, Pennsylvania. He was a cute little fellow who looked a lot like his brother and sister. Sarah was helpful to her mother in the care of Malcolm. She was also becoming a good cook, making cookies and birthday cakes for her family members. She was taking dancing lessons and was scheduled to dance in a recital later that month. She was also active in Brownies.

Summer at Rockport that year was filled with visits from grandchildren and their families. Sarah was a good swimmer and Kristen and Cortlandt also learned to swim that summer. They enjoyed jumping the waves at the beach, as well as swimming and diving off our rocks. Bearskin Neck continued to be a favorite place to visit especially the Country Store with its penny candy. We usually stopped at Cathy and Rick's house on our way to and from Rockport. They were most gracious to us and Cathy almost always made my favorite dessert, bread pudding with whipped cream.

At the end of June when we stopped in Danbury Carrie was sixteen months old. She continued to amaze us with her precocity. She was eager to show us how she could type her name on the computer. She continued to enjoy having books read to her and she liked to walk down to the pond near her house to feed the ducks. She could sing several nursery rhymes such as *Twinkle Twinkle Little Star* and some simple hymns.

All of our children and their families were together at Rockport in August. Cindy, Denis and their boys came first. We caught up on the news of Thomas and Lucas as soon as they arrived. Thomas had had a very successful baseball season with his team, the Eagles. He had made ten hits during the season and was very enthusiastic about the sport. He was signed up to play on a soccer team in the fall. Thomas was an excellent athlete. He was a fast runner with a great deal of determination. This helped him become a successful soccer player in the fall. Lucas had enjoyed being home with his parents while Thomas was in school. He was a happy talkative little fellow with a twinkle in his eye and a continual smile on his face. He liked to jump up and down when he was excited, which was frequently. He was also very curious and continually asked, "Why?"

Steve drove up with his family the day after the Lavoies arrived. When Steve pulled into the driveway we all went out to meet him and his family. Thomas and Lucas had not seen them for almost a year. Kristen jumped out of the van and ran up to

Thomas, as they had always been great buddies. Janice, Steve and Nicole all got out and then Victoria with her beautiful golden curly hair stepped out of the van and smiled at Lucas. He was immediately smitten. He took her hand and they walked off into the yard together. How I wished that I had a camera at that moment.

The grandchildren thoroughly enjoyed playing together. The older children like to explore the bushes and find hideouts. Victoria, Nicole, Lucas and Carrie enjoyed playing in the little playhouse and having tea parties on the children's picnic table. All the children liked to play on the jungle gym in my cousin's yard. Of course swimming and Bearskin Neck were popular with all of them. Every afternoon after lunch Janice took the younger children for a ride in her van to put them to sleep for a nap. For these rides we called her van the "napmobile."

All three of my brothers and their families were in Rockport that August. Mike took some good pictures of my brothers and me sitting together at the dining room table. We had a great time playing games together and swimming across the cove. Bunkie and I swam out to an island and sat on seaweed covered rocks reminiscing about our childhood as we looked out at the beautiful scenery. Mike and I invited all the relatives to a big picnic, but it rained; so, instead, we had a buffet dinner at the house for the forty-five guests. We rented a large grill and the boys cooked meat on the far end of the porch. Cindy and Peter made a huge fresh fruit salad and the Gordon family brought food also. There seemed to be plenty of room for everyone in the house. People sat on the porch, in the living room and along the dining room walls. The teenagers sat in our new playroom and talked and watched television. A week later we hosted a party for thirty-four guests for Sarah's seventh birthday.

Towards the end of August Mike and I were invited to a fiftieth anniversary party for Emily and Dick Gordon. It was limited to their family, but they consider us as family. It was a lovely party held in the upstairs of a popular restaurant in town called My Place. The cocktails were on a porch overlooking the ocean and the dinner was inside. The Gordon children gave out quizzes about the marriage of their parents and family photo albums were passed around. David and Mary were there and everyone was asked to tell how they were related to Emily and Dick. Mike explained that he was related by being married to me and I was the sister of Emily's sister's husband. That got them so confused that no one questioned him further. We had a wonderful time!

Mike and I celebrated Labor Day weekend alone. We went out to dinner every evening and saw a number of good movies. We stopped at Cathy and Rick's house on the way home and enjoyed a delicious dinner. Carrie delighted in singing all the words to a number of children's songs and regaled us with tales of her activities. She loved to spin round in circles and never seemed to get dizzy. After dinner we read her several books and proceeded on our way.

We spent the next two weeks in Bound Brook and witnessed the horror of September 11 on television. One of my friends from the registrar's office at Wagner lost her son in that disaster. She was on a trip in Italy and saw her son's building go down on television. She couldn't get a plane back to the United States and suffered agony in Italy for several days before she could go home. What a terrible tragedy! We attended the memorial service for her son on Staten Island.

At the end of September Steve and Janice invited us to join their family at the annual balloon festival at Solberg Airport. The airport was down the street from their house. We parked in a field and a school bus transported us to the airport. Victoria and Nicole were excited about riding on a school bus as they envied Kristen riding in one to kindergarten every day. When we reached the festival we sat on the grass and watched people inflate their balloons and take off into the sky. The balloons were bright and colorful and we saw some new specially shaped ones, including an eagle, a mail truck and a cowboy hat. The girls took a simulated ride in a balloon that was tethered to the ground but gave the effect of rising into the air and descending back to the ground. The next morning Steve's family saw the balloons again as they flew over their yard in a race as the second event of the balloon festival.

On November 11th we traveled with Steve's family to Lancaster for Malcolm's christening. We treated Steve, Janice and their children to a motel room adjacent to ours at the Hampton Inn and we all enjoyed the free evening cocoa and morning breakfast together. We ate breakfast beside the outdoor pool while the children ran round and round the fence enclosing the pool. At the church service Pete and Dorianne took all their children up to the altar for the christening ceremony. Malcolm was adorable when the minister baptized him and Sarah and Cortlandt were very well behaved. There was a nice reception at their house after the service.

On Thanksgiving the family, except for the Lavoies, came to our house. We invited Bruce McCreary to join us, as he was alone for the holiday. We had a big turkey and the children all enjoyed playing together after dinner. We had one mishap when Carrie spun so much that she became dizzy and fell into the corner of the coffee table. Cathy and Rick took her to the emergency room and were gone for two hours. We saved their dinner and when they returned Carrie had several stitches in her forehead, but the experience had not curbed her exuberance.

On the first of December, Steve and his family moved into the house of Janice's mother in Manville, New Jersey. When her mother died she left her house to Janice and her brother, John. John had been living with his mother before she died and he continued to live in the house after her death. He paid Janice a monthly rent while he lived there. He and his girlfriend, Heidi, had been looking for a house of their own and when they found a place that they liked, John moved out of his mother's house and Janice and her family moved in. She and Steve paid John for his half of the house. Janice had always wanted to return to Manville and she was thrilled to move into the house of her childhood.

The house was a good size for their family. There were two good-sized bedrooms and a bath on the second floor; a large living room, modern kitchen, a dining area, two more bedrooms and bath on the first floor; and three rooms in a finished basement. Kristen transferred from her first grade class in Whitehouse Station into a class at Weston School in Manville. At first she missed her old class and she kept in touch with her former teacher, who thought very highly of her. But she adapted well to her new class and began to make new friends.

On December 14th we attended a concert in Rick's church. Cathy had invited her former church choir in Hempstead to give a concert in Danbury. Cathy's church in Hempstead had a black congregation. The choir members had powerful voices and their concert was inspiring. Rick's church provided a dinner in the social hall before the concert so we had a chance to meet Cathy's friends. In the sanctuary the choir members asked Cathy to sing a solo while they hummed in the background. Cathy let her voice out with a full crescendo and it brought tears to my eyes as I heard her magnificent singing.

We also went to hear Kristen sing in her school program. Victoria had helped Kristen practice and had learned *God Bless America* herself in the process. During the school program the audience was asked to join in the singing of *God Bless America*. Victoria sang all the words louder than anyone else in the audience. The lady in front of her was amazed when she turned around and saw little two-and-a-half-year-old Victoria belting out the song.

We visited Cindy and Denis the week before Christmas. My brother Bunkie, his wife, Ann, and their daughters, Heather and Andrea, who lived in Washington State, joined us for dinner. They had brought presents so we were able to have an exchange of gifts. Bunkie gave me *Seabiscuit,* which turned out to be a favorite book for Mike, Peter and me. We played charades after dinner and Thomas proved to be a good little actor. It was great to have so many family members together in Seattle. We came home in time to celebrate Christmas with the rest of our children and grandchildren on December 26th.

We started off the New Year of 2002 by having Steve and Janice and their children to dinner on New Year's Day. We saw their family frequently during January. Brad was always happy to see us when we visited his house. He was usually standing in his playpen watching television when we came in the front door. When he saw us he would squeal with glee and raise his arms to be picked up. He was such a loving child and would hug me for several minutes before he was put down. He and Nicole seemed to have a strong bond between them. If he saw her lying on the floor crying he would crawl over to her, turn her over and put a pacifier in her mouth.

Victoria aligned herself with Kristen. She stated that she was a big girl like Kristen and she wanted to do everything Kristen did. Usually Kristen would accept Victoria's adoration, but once in a while she would send her away, which would devastate Victoria. Whenever Victoria was upset she would hold "Dolly Wolly" up to her face and suck her thumb. "Dolly Wolly" was a bedraggled terrycloth doll, which was once pink but had been gray for a long time. She had lost most of her stuffing, but if she was not around at crucial times Victoria was inconsolable. The "binky", a.k.a., pacifier, was of equal importance to Nicole. Whenever we took the twins to the park we made sure we had both of these mollifiers with us. On their birthday, we gave Nicole and Victoria a party at our house. We gave them each a tricycle. Nicole, who was bolder than Victoria, immediately began to ride her new tricycle but it took Victoria several months before she would try hers.

Kristen joined the Brownies in the second half of the first grade and enjoyed making new friends and participating in new activities. Cortlandt joined the Cub Scouts about the same time. In February Kristen was chosen from her class to receive the *Student of the Month Award,* and she also won the *Math and Science Award.* We were so proud of her for such achievements only two months after she started a new school. Mike and I were impressed with the support that Weston School gave Kristen as a new student.

Manville has a charming small town atmosphere. The town sponsors parades, holiday activities and excellent sports activities. At Easter time the town provides egg hunts for the children and, for the fourth of July and Christmas, there are parades in which the townspeople participate. There are town carnivals with games, rides and refreshments once or twice a year and, in the summer, the town pool is popular with the residents. Manville sponsors sports teams in the spring and fall for the children and the library holds a story time each week for small children. Kristen, Victoria and Nicole managed to have their pictures in the local paper a number of times as the various local activities are frequently featured.

On February 23rd Janice hosted a party at her house for the twins and Brad. Cathy, Rick and Carrie came as well as Peter and Dorianne's family. Uncle John gave Victoria and Nicole a microphone and all the children enjoyed singing into it. Some of them were quite dramatic in their performances. There were favors, many gifts to be opened and a cake for each of them. Sarah and Victoria played together upstairs after dinner and the other children sat holding their balloons in the living room glued to the television.

On the night of the party, Peter's family slept at our house and the next morning we took his family and Steve's to George's Restaurant for brunch. George's Restaurant was originally the Bound Brook Railroad Station. George rented the building and decorated it with murals of trains and toy trains for customers to look at or play with. We had the back room to ourselves and the grandchildren had a great time playing with the toy trains and watching the real trains stopping outside the window.

The next family birthday party was for Carrie in Danbury. Kristen came with us to the party. Cathy had planned some imaginative games including having the children march around the house with noisemakers. The children designed their own hats and made the noisemakers. Kristen enjoyed making pictures with all the crayons and paper. Cathy had baked a big cake with green icing and Carrie blew out the candles.

Mike and I spent Easter with Peter's family in Lancaster. We went to church with them and then shared a delicious ham dinner with them at their house. Sarah, Cortlandt and Malcolm looked very handsome in their new Easter outfits. I took many snapshots of them. We celebrated Cathy's birthday a week later at our house with Steve's and Peter's families and Ralph Pritchard. It was fun watching the grandchildren play and Cathy open her gifts. On Mother's Day we had our annual big celebration at Ellery's restaurant. In June Peter's and Cathy's families joined us in a celebration of Steve's birthday. Mike bought some large balls and other games to keep the grandchildren busy in our back yard.

Steve, Peter and Cathy traveled to Rockport with their families for the fourth of July festivities. We had a fun filled summer with many visits from family and friends. Cindy's family came east for three weeks in August and all the grandchildren were glad to see Thomas and Lucas again. They divided up as big kids and little kids again, but this time Victoria decided that she

was a "big kid" and refused to go with the younger children in
the "napmobile." She tried to keep up with the older children
and they were receptive to her most of the time. One time,
however, they all climbed up a steep rock, which she could not
climb, leaving her behind. Mike went looking for her and found
her standing at the bottom of the rock, sad but not crying. Nicole
was perfectly happy to play with Lucas and Carrie who were
her age. The following week my brother David and his wife,
Mary, joined us. We played many games together and David
and I swam across the cove together every day. We had our
usual picnics with all the relatives and the Gordon family. Our
last gathering of the summer at Rockport was with Steve's family
over Labor Day weekend.

We finished the year with Thanksgiving at Carol and Steve's
house in Rockville, Maryland and Christmas at our house. We
treated Steve's and Peter's families to motel rooms on
Thanksgiving night so that they did not have to return home
that day and could stay and play games with Carol, Steve and
their children. At the motel the rooms were suites with living
rooms and kitchens. The grandchildren loved jumping on all
the beds in their two-room-suites and falling asleep while
watching the free videos from the desk. The motel provided
free breakfasts and we all met in the dining room for a plentiful
buffet in the morning. We then packed our bags and headed
over to Carol's house for lunch before we drove back home. It
was a great holiday celebration.

We celebrated Christmas with three out of four of our children
and their families in Bound Brook. On December 27, 2002 our
eleventh grandchild, Braden Beckford Schuyler was born. We
drove to Lancaster to see him that day and he was adorable,
just as his brothers and sister had been. The next day we
celebrated a late Christmas with Peter and Dorianne and their
family at the hospital. The hospital had a unique system of
transporting patient's belongings when they left the hospital.

They used big red children's wagons with high sides so that nothing would fall out. We took one of the wagons to our car and loaded it up with the Christmas gifts that we had brought. We had a joyful celebration together in Dorianne's hospital room opening all the gifts.

Mike and I stayed for three days and nights in a fancy resort hotel in Lancaster thanks to a public relations program that Peter had spotted in the local paper. The resort offered free rooms to the grandparents of babies born in the area between December 15th and January 15th. The rooms were free as long as the babies were in the hospital. We had a beautiful room and were able to visit Braden and his family every day.

We now have eleven little grandchildren and two older step-grandchildren. They are very precious to us. Our children tell us that this is the final number of grandchildren that we will have and we think that we are extremely fortunate grandparents to have so many wonderful children to love. Each child is unique.

Sarah is a beautiful child with blonde hair, blue eyes and a lovely smile. She always wants to do the right thing and to please others. She has struggled with this desire as she has an excess of energy that she can not always control. When she was small she frequently got into mischief and at times she flailed out at other children. Cortlandt came into her family when she was two years old and she demonstrated strong sibling rivalry towards him. However, she has been very caring for her other younger brothers who arrived at a less threatening time in her life. When Sarah was in kindergarten and first grade she had difficulty concentrating. Her parents sought professional advice on how to help her. Peter approached the school board about sending her to a private school. The board declined to do this, but instead, arranged for a teacher's helper to support Sarah in the regular classroom.

Sarah responded well to Mrs. Rineer, the aid who worked with
her. Mrs. Rineer taught Sarah how to relate to others and how
to direct her energy in constructive ways. Sarah's attitude and
grades improved remarkably under her tutelage. She now does
very well in her schoolwork. On her last report card she received
all A's. She also has made a number of new friends. Sarah has
visited us alone on several occasions and has been a delightful
guest. She is a very loving child and Mike and I always enjoy
being with her.

Thomas is a handsome young boy with straight yellow hair,
blue eyes and a big smile. After a harrowing start in life, he
became an energetic and cheerful little boy who developed
into an enthusiastic and determined child. He is a successful
athlete and has been an active member of a baseball team, the
Eagles, and of a soccer team, the Mighty Green Mellonheads,
for several years. He has an excellent scoring record on both
teams. He likes to build intricate machines with Lego and K-
Nex, often using the computer to help him design them. He
also likes to play racing games on the computer, but has a time
limit set by his parents on this activity.

Thomas pursues projects with intense interest and is a leader
among his friends. He draws other children to him because of
his creative ideas and his intensity in carrying them out. Thomas
enjoys reading and has read all five of the Harry Potter books.
He also enjoys having Grandpa read to him when we visit Seattle.
Thomas has been a thoughtful and considerate big brother to Lucas,
but this became a little more difficult when Lucas became more
independent and developed a mind of his own. Thomas thoroughly
enjoys his visits with his cousins at Rockport. Kristen especially
appreciates all his jokes and his creative ideas.

Kristen is a beautiful young girl with thick brown wavy hair
and big blue eyes. She has a sweet and loving nature. She is
caring and kind to her younger sisters and brother and helpful

to her mother and father. She enjoys shopping with her dad and confiding in her mom during their bedtime chats. She enjoys writing in her journal and using her mother's computer to write stories and play games. She likes to visit her grandparents on weekends. She goes on adventures with Nana and writes poems and letters to her cousins on Grandpa's computer. She plays games with both grandparents and makes cookies with Nana. She loves to run and joins her dad and grandpa when they play tennis so she can chase the balls for them. She has enjoyed playing on the Manville girls' soccer team.

Kristen is very conscientious about her schoolwork and achieves all "A's" on her report card. She has received rave reviews from her teachers and school administrators. Her principal at Weston School described her as "cooperative, patient, caring and eager to please." He added, "She takes great pride in her work and her smile and cheerful personality brighten the classroom." This is an accurate description of Kristen. She participates regularly in school recitals. On one occasion she was chosen to read her poem in a school assembly. She told me that she was very nervous, but she performed well. She was selected for the Gifted and Talented Program in her school and enjoys doing projects with her friend Nicole, who is also in the program.

Kristen has won contests in the community as well as at school. She won an award for a poster on safety and another for a poster about dental care. The prize for the latter was six tickets to the Barnum and Bailey Circus. She and her family had a great time at the circus. She was taken on a tour of the dressing rooms and allowed to go into the center ring before the show began. Kristen has visited us alone for weeks at Rockport and has been a wonderful guest. She is a delightful child and has brought immense joy to her family.

Cortlandt was a beautiful baby with an unusually large head. He was good-natured from the beginning. Early on, when

Sarah would trash the living room with toys, he would methodically pick up every toy and put it back where it came from. He developed into an extroverted little boy who easily made friends. He was single-minded in his interests. He went from being obsessed with Thomas the Tank Engine, to fascination with the Titanic, to intense interest in dinosaurs and finally he became an avid collector of baseball cards. He became an expert in each one of these interests. Cortlandt has a very inquisitive mind and continually asks perceptive questions.

Cortlandt does very well in his schoolwork. He earned recognition as the best reader in his class for two years in a row. He was chosen, along with six other first and second graders in his school, to participate in the Odyssey of the Mind Program for outstanding students. He has been active in Cub Scouts and has made many friends in the organization, including his best friend, Ian. In Lancaster he enjoys swimming, wrestling and riding his bike. Cortlandt is a very friendly child. He thinks up creative games to play with his cousins at Rockport and keeps them entertained with his enthusiastic chatter. He has made several visits to our homes in Bound Brook and Rockport and has always been a pleasure to be with.

Nicole is a lovely little girl with wispy blonde hair, rosy cheeks and rosebud lips. When she smiles her whole face lights up. She loves candy but is not too fond of regular food. Lately, however, she has taken a liking to baked potatoes and will eat two at a sitting. She is enthusiastic and loving and whenever we go into her house she runs up to us and jumps into our arms. She demonstrates determination, but she is also sensitive to criticism and will burst into tears if her feelings are hurt.

Nicole is adventuresome and will try new challenges, such as big slides and new bikes, without hesitation. She is very independent. When Kristen and Victoria ask her why she will not join them in an activity, she replies, "I do what I want to do." She is also persistent. When she wants something, especially candy, she will not stop asking for it. Or if she wants you to listen to her, she will continue to talk to you until you give her your undivided attention. She is interested in new things and asks a lot of questions in school and at home about her interests. She makes friends easily and is devoted to them once she has befriended them. Nicole is a very affectionate and interesting child. She is a joy to be with.

Victoria is a charming little girl with blonde curly hair and a winning smile. She is warm and friendly and likes to be cuddled. When she was younger she used to want me to hold her. Now she likes Grandpa to hold her too. She has quite an imagination and likes to pretend that she is baking cookies on our toy stove. She also calls her friends on the toy telephone and asks them to dinner. When she is playing a game with us she will excuse herself to check if the cookies are done. She is cautious about trying new activities and very sensitive if criticized. She has a stubborn streak, which usually comes out when it is time to leave and she is having a good time. She is a fan of Ariel in Walt Disney's *Little Mermaid* movie and brings one or two Ariel dolls, as well as Dolly Wolly, wherever she goes.

Victoria worships her big sister, Kristen and wants to do everything that she does. She even asks what color vitamin Kristen took so that she can have the same color. She considers herself a big girl and wants to play with Kristen and her older cousins. She likes to be with people and follow what others are doing. She is responsible and reports threatening situations immediately to adults. She enjoys wearing pretty dresses and comes to church in her prettiest party dresses on Sundays. She enjoys both her Sunday school and her school classes and is well liked by her teachers. Victoria is a charming and loving little girl and it is always a pleasure to have her visit us.

Lucas is an adorable little boy with blonde curly hair, blue eyes and a wonderful smile. He is full of energy and talks incessantly. He has a bubbly personality and is very extroverted. He jumps up and down a lot and asks lots of questions. "Why" is one of his favorite words. When he was two and three years old he was full of mischief and Thomas referred to him as "Destructo." As he grew older he stopped getting into things and just concentrated on befriending others. When he first attended pre-school he had a short attention span and the teacher told his parents that he had trouble focusing. He not only could not focus, but he prevented the rest of the class from focusing, as he always wanted to talk to everyone. He does much better in school now and enjoys going all day so he can take his lunch with him just as Thomas does. Mike and I find Lucas to be a delightful cuddly little boy who shows us a great deal of love and cheerfulness. It is always fun to be with him.

Carrie is a darling little girl with honey colored hair, sparkling eyes and a delightful giggle. She is an enthusiastic, happy child who brightens every corner of a room. Her mother nursed her for four years so she never needed a pacifier when she was upset. She is a very smart child who learned her letters when she was one and soon afterwards spelled her name. She loves to read books and have them read to her. She has always enjoyed singing with her parents and big sisters. She learned the words to many hymns and children's songs early on.

Carrie is an optimistic little girl who likes to tell you about all the good things that are going to happen to her. She is also independent and likes to think that she can handle things by herself. This frequently leads to a bit of stubbornness when it comes to doing what she should instead of what she wants. She likes to paint, swim, jump, go to gymnastics and ride on the carousel. She also has a full schedule of church and pre-school activities. She enjoys playing with the many imaginative toys at home, church and pre-school. Carrie is a delight to visit or have as a guest in our house.

Brad is a charming little boy with beautiful brown hair, bluish green eyes and a continual smile. He is a child that you can't help loving. He is always cheerful and he has a loving nature. He hugs all the relatives and is always delighted to see Mike and me when we visit his house. He is always happy, laughing and eager to do something with us. When we take him to the park he climbs on all the play equipment and makes friends easily with the other children. He is such a contented child that he never needed a pacifier. He has three older sisters who adore him and treat him kindly. He is so happy that it is difficult for anyone to be cross with him. The only time he ever cries is if he thinks someone is criticizing him. However no one needs to criticize him, as he is so pleasant to be around.

When Brad's sisters were all in school, his mother took him out every morning and that made him happier than ever to have her undivided attention. He started pre-school in the spring of 2004 and thoroughly enjoys it. He now wears a backpack of his own and feels very important. He likes his friends in pre-school and has learned some songs. All of Brad's relatives feel fortunate to have such a wonderful little boy in the family and that includes Mike and me.

Malcolm is a tough little boy. He has blonde hair, blue eyes and a determined look on his face. When he is excited he has a great big smile! Like his brother, Cortlandt, he is single minded in his interests. Currently his obsession in life is trucks. He has many trucks but is not happy about sharing these with his baby brother, Braden. When Malcolm's little brother started to crawl, Malcolm would yell, "No baby," if he moved toward his trucks. When Braden grew a little bigger, Malcolm considered him fair game for wrestling. When they were at a playground Malcolm wouldn't let other children come near Braden. He kept repeating, "My baby, my baby." When the other children backed off Malcolm resumed wrestling with Braden. I guess he was telling them that Braden was his baby to wrestle.

Malcolm likes to visit us and play with the matchbox trucks we have. He calls us on the phone and says, "Go see Pop Pop and play with trucks." He is a cute little boy and behaves very well when he visits us. We took him to church and he sat in Mike's lap through the entire service. He didn't make a sound until the minister said that he would only talk for a few minutes more. In a loud voice Malcolm said, "Uh-oh." The church audience laughed. That same weekend we took Malcolm to the carnival in Manville and he enjoyed jumping in the moonwalk. Malcolm is fond of his cousin Brad and hugs him each time he sees him. They enjoy playing together and rarely fight. Malcolm is a happy child and we really enjoy having him visit us.

Braden is a cheerful little toddler. He is a beautiful child with blond wispy hair, blue eyes, pink cheeks and a winning smile. He loves to be held by grownups, as most babies do. He adores his big brother Malcolm and follows him everywhere in spite of the rough treatment he receives from him. He rarely cries when Malcolm wrestles with him, but he has already learned to pull Malcolm's hair to defend himself. Recently Malcolm appears to be giving him more respect. Sarah gives Braden lots of love and tries to protect him from his big brother. His parents adore him and so do we.

19

Retirement

Mike and I decided to retire in 2001 so that we could spend more time with each other and with our grandchildren. He retired on April 30th and I retired on the last day of June. Beverly Weber gave Mike a retirement party at her house at the end of April. It was a marvelous affair. Our whole family was present, as were many of Mike's colleagues, business clients and other friends. Each of our children gave a touching speech about Mike as a father. Cindy wrote a lovely poem about her father and presented it to him in an attractive frame after the party. June 22nd was the date of the surprise party for my retirement. Several other retirement parties were given for me at Wagner College, but none of them could compare to the one that Mike and the children gave me. Cindy also wrote a beautiful poem for me. June 29th was my last day of work. Mike came to Wagner and, after the last party in the Registrar's Office, he and I packed up all my belongings and moved me out of my office.

We wasted no time in implementing our plan to spend more time with our children and grandchildren. I spent the rest of the summer at Rockport without worrying about proofreading bulletins or hurrying back to Wagner College to work on some project. We started a new system for the grandchildren at Rockport. We invited each of the older grandchildren to spend a week alone with us so that we could give each one our undivided attention. Sarah came first. I took her to the beach and to Bearskin Neck and Mike took her climbing on the rocks. We both read to her and she and I cooked pancakes together for breakfast. We so enjoyed giving our full attention to Sarah and she responded with joy and enthusiasm. After the week was up we took Sarah back to Lancaster and picked up Cortlandt for his visit.

We enjoyed Cortlandt's visit and did special activities with him. The Titanic was no longer his major interest: he had become an expert on dinosaurs. He knew facts about all types of dinosaurs and in what era they lived. He could spell the names of the different eras and of the beasts that lived in each one. He kept a journal in his class and filled it with facts about these animals and, for his class project, he built a model of Tyrannosaurus Rex with help from his father. At Rockport we read to him about dinosaurs and he used his allowance to buy several toy dinosaurs at The Toy Store on Bearskin Neck. Cortlandt was a good rock climber and enjoyed exploring for caves in the rocks with Mike. While he was with us we had a visit from my secretary at Wagner, Ann Dillon. Her husband, Dick, is six feet five inches tall and looked like a giant next to Cortlandt. I took some cute pictures of them together. Dick liked Cortlandt and bought him a toy fishing boat. Following Cortlandt's visit, Steve and his family came up for the weekend. Steve and Mike left for New Jersey on Sunday night while Janice and the children stayed on for a week with me. We went to the beach every day.

Kristen came for her week alone with us during the first week of August. She loved going to the beach with me. She jumped the waves and ran up and down the beach to warm up. There was a cute puppy at the beach one day and she had a wonderful time running and playing with it. She liked to visit Mimi and her daughter, Elizabeth, at their house next door. Elizabeth let her use her computer and Kristen liked playing with the toys at their house. Steve, Janice and the rest of their children came back to Rockport and took Kristen home at the end of the weekend.

Cindy and her family arrived early in August. Steve's and Cathy's families arrived soon afterwards and Peter came a little later as did my brother Bunkie and his wife. We had a number of dinners and parties and it was a festive two weeks. Everyone left Rockport the third weekend of the month including Mike and me. We returned to Rockport the next weekend and I stayed for another week as Mildred Nelson joined me for the last week of August.

In September Mike, Rick and Steve cut down brush and trees next to the house and took several loads to the dump in Steve's truck. My uncle, Bob Smith, came to visit us while we were there. He was 89 years old and he usually stayed a very short time when he came. I coaxed him into the dining room and gave him croissants and coffee. He stayed for a couple of hours and seemed to enjoy himself. When he left he said that he would be back. He came back two days later and brought us a number of books. He was clearing out his house as he was preparing to sell it and move into a retirement complex. His wife, Margaret, had been in a nursing home for several years and he no longer wanted to live alone in his house. He is my father's youngest brother and the last living sibling. He still was very spry with a great sense of humor and we enjoyed his visits immensely. We had not seen a great deal of him over the years as he and his family had their summer home in Marshfield, Massachusetts, not in Rockport with the rest of his relatives. During the rest of September I swam every day and on the 30th we closed the house for the winter.

During the last year of his business, Mike had planned to start a newsletter for the four older grandchildren after he retired. He decided to call it *Tidings*. He prepared the first issue in the month after he retired and mailed it out at the end of June. *Tidings* was eight pages long and included seven different sections. The first section told what was special about the month. The masthead included pictures of the four older grandchildren. The second section described the activities of the four grandchildren during the prior month. The third section was about a person or event in history and the fourth one was on poetry. The fifth section described some place in America. The sixth section related a legend or myth and the last section was about natural science. Most sections of *Tidings* were on one page, but the section with the longest write-up was two pages. Each page had a number of colored pictures to illustrate the text.

To prepare *Tidings* each month I visited our local library and took out about fifteen books with writing and pictures about the topics that we had chosen to present that month. Mike wrote his own version of the stories for the various sections and I supplied him with the information and the pictures to complete each page. Through experimentation Mike learned how to format the sections and scan the pictures onto the pages. When we finished the eight pages we took them to a copy center to be printed on eleven by seventeen-inch glossy paper, that was folded and stapled to make an eight-page booklet.

Each month the topics for the first page of *Tidings* included family celebrations as well as special holidays or historical events that happened in that month. For example, in February there were birthdays for Nicole, Victoria, Brad, Carrie and Julie, and the special holidays included Lincoln's and Washington's birthdays, Black History Month and Valentine's Day. We usually described one of the special holidays or events and included a picture related to it at the bottom of the page.

The second section of *Tidings* was entitled "Kinformation." This section reported on the activities that Sarah, Thomas, Kristen and Cortlandt were involved in each month. I called each grandchild for a report on his or her activities during the month before I wrote this section. Sarah's activities included dancing, cooking, swimming, reading, school projects, field trips, Brownies, birthday celebrations and helping care for her baby brothers. Thomas' favorite activities were baseball and soccer and he also liked to hike and go kayaking on camping trips with his family. He liked reading and spelling and his favorite hobby was creating vehicles and monsters with his Lego and K-nex sets.

Kristen liked to cook, swim and play soccer. She enjoyed playing with Disney figurines at Nana's house and writing stories on Grandpa's computer. She liked to write in her journal and was an outstanding student in school, where she won a number of awards and prizes. Cortlandt was interested in dinosaurs at first. He liked to visit museums with displays of dinosaurs and he read many books about them. Later he became interested in baseball, collecting cards and attending games. He enjoyed swimming and wrestling and joined the Cub Scouts where he made many friends.

On the "Kinformation" page there were pictures of each child doing one of the activities described. I took some of the pictures and asked their parents to send us some. This section was the children's favorite; they always turned to it immediately on receiving *Tidings*. In months where there was a great deal of activity, such as August, October or December, we frequently enlarged this section to two pages with a gallery of pictures on one of the pages.

The third section of *Tidings* was called "Long, Long Ago." In this section we presented stories about historical figures or events. There were stories of presidents, explorers, inventors, religious leaders, civil rights leaders, athletes, authors and people in medicine. Historical events covered the gamut from famous battles to one-room schools. Of all the famous people that were reported during the first three years six were women, which, in my opinion, was not enough. Of course Florence Nightingale was one of these. Section four was the "Poetry Page." The poem frequently related to the topic in another section of the same month's edition. Poems were about children, animals, birds, trees, famous people, holidays, seasons of the year and humor. I found pictures to illustrate the poems and the grandchildren enjoyed memorizing some of them.

Section five contained descriptions and stories about "America the Beautiful." As of June 2004 we have reported on twenty states, seven large cities, five national parks, the Great Lakes and the Mississippi River. Our local library has a series of books about the states in the country. We used these books frequently in our reports about the states. Also, my grandmother gave me a beautiful book on the National Parks that has been a great help in illustrating this section. The sixth section is entitled "Tales of Yore." We have especially enjoyed choosing and writing about the myths and stories for this section. We have used American, Greek and Asian myths, plus Aesop's Fables and other stories from history and literature. We own a number of excellent books on myths and cultural tales and some of the best stories came from my father's home reader published in the 1890's.

The final section of *Tidings* is called "Mother Nature." In this section we have written about different areas of science and nature such as astronomy, animals, flowers, human anatomy, trees and weather. Some of the natural phenomena that we have described include lightning, tornadoes, tsunamis, volcanoes and wetlands. It has been a challenge to find good pictures of all these. Each month one section lends itself to a longer write-up, so it is to that section that we devote our extra page.

When we first started *Tidings*, we asked each of the four grandchildren to prepare a report on their state for the "America the Beautiful" section. Cortlandt and Thomas also wrote reports for the section, "Mother Nature." Thomas wrote and illustrated a report on the solar system and Cortlandt wrote a report on dinosaurs. After that they left the writing to Nana and Grandpa. *Tidings* became popular not only with the grandchildren, but also with their parents and other adults who read it. Each month it takes us a full week or more to prepare *Tidings* but we thoroughly enjoy the task. We have continued to write and publish it monthly even when burdened with sickness or major events. We are now developing a game of *Tidings Trivia* for the grandchildren to play.

Another project that Mike decided on before our retirement was to take up square dancing again. We had enjoyed this activity thirty years before when we were living in the Philippines, but found that our work and family schedules were too full to continue it after we returned to the States. After we retired we found a square dance group that meets in Bound Brook. However they informed us that we would have to take a year of lessons before we could join their group. Undaunted by this news, we signed up for lessons that began in the fall of 2001. We remembered a few moves from thirty years before, but we realized that we had a great deal to learn.

The people in our square dance class were very nice and we soon made lots of new friends. To make our learning easier a group of expert square dancers from the sponsoring club, the Bee Sharps, volunteered their time to dance with us and help us follow the calls. They were called "angels", an appropriate name for helpers. After we finished our year of training, we also became angels. We took lessons every Monday evening and progressed through two levels of dancing called "mainstream" and "plus." We received graduation diplomas and became official members of the Bee Sharps in May 2002. One of the angel couples invited both angels and students to their home for a Christmas party at the end of the mainstream training. We got to know all the dancers even better there and had a jolly time.

One of the activities that the Bee Sharps occasionally conduct is a "raid," when members from our club raid another club's dance. During the evening the raiding club marches into the dance hall and gives a cheer. Members of our club carry stuffed toy bees and wear bee antennae on their heads. Each club has specific colors and its members wear those colors on the night of the raid. Our club colors are red and black.

Being retired allowed us time to participate in activities such as square dancing and it also allowed us to help our children when they needed us. In October 2001 we took Sarah and Cortlandt for four days to give Dorianne a break and, later in the month, when Cathy needed to have a knee operation, I took care of Carrie while she recuperated. I stayed with her for two weeks, going home to be with Mike on the weekends when Rick could take care of her. While I was in Danbury I took Carrie for walks, read to her and played games with her. I drove Cathy to the physical therapist and helped with the shopping and cooking. After Carrie and her parents went to bed I re-read Katherine Graham's autobiography in preparation for my presentation to the Deipnos the night that I returned home. It was most enjoyable being able to spend so much time with Carrie and her parents.

Retirement gave us the opportunity to spend time with grandchildren during the week. Mike and I took Victoria and Nicole to the park once each week and Kristen spent some time with us every weekend and an occasional afternoon after school. We had a regular routine with Nicole and Victoria. First we stopped at Dunkin' Donuts for lunch, then we drove to the park where they climbed on the playground equipment and walked down to the pond to see the ducks. After we left the park we stopped at the ice-cream parlor for cones and rides on the mechanical horse in the front of the store. I sat with Brad and the twins sometimes while Janice did errands or got a haircut. Mike and I were also able to attend school programs during the week. We attended Kristen's concert at Weston School in Manville, Sarah and Cortlandt's Christmas concert in Lancaster and Thomas' concert when we visited his family before Christmas in Seattle. We also attended Thomas' piano recital when we were there.

Early in December 2001 I suggested to Mike that we go on a short vacation of our own before Christmas. Mike said that we couldn't just go on a vacation on the spur of the moment and I retorted, "Why not, we're retired." He had to agree with me and we drove down to Cape May for a few days. We stayed at the Hotel Lafayette overlooking the ocean where we enjoyed a free breakfast each day. We found a charming little outdoor shopping mall two blocks from our hotel and did our Christmas shopping for the distant relatives. We bought fifty-five gifts and our favorite stores were a Swedish lace shop and a discount bookstore. On our last evening in Cape May we had dinner at an elegant Victorian inn and decided that it would be a perfect place for a Deipnos get-together in the spring. We came back to Bound Brook in time to drive to Lancaster and take Peter to dinner for his birthday on December 7th.

At the beginning of 2002 Mike and I decided to go on a diet together. We were both thirty pounds overweight. Mike believes in keeping detailed records so he devised a chart for us to record our progress. Every day of the week was shown on the chart with tiny boxes to record how many calories we ate for breakfast, morning snack, lunch, two afternoon snacks, dinner and an evening snack. My aim was to consume no more than 900 calories per day and Mike's goal was no more than 1200 calories per day. The chart also included spaces to record daily exercises and weight. In four and a half months I dropped 25 pounds and Mike lost 23. In the next few months I lost another eight pounds for a total of 33. We were very pleased with ourselves and managed to maintain our weight loss by continuing to record our calories. Mike's maintenance calorie load is 1500 calories a day and mine is 1200. We did not follow any prescribed diet, we just learned to eat moderately.

In February Mike decided that our house needed a little sprucing up. We painted the kitchen and then ordered a new Corian counter top. Mike had promised me a new counter when we moved into the house in 1962, as the pink counter clashed with the yellow walls and blue and white delft decorations. However he never seemed to get around to changing the counter. By this time the original stove had only one burner functioning and that burner had to be turned on with a pair of pliers. Retirement seemed to be a good time to refurbish the kitchen. In addition to a new counter and sink, we bought a new stovetop. To top it off Mike suggested that we also order a new floor. We found a beautiful porcelain tile and a nice young man to install it. We finally had a gorgeous kitchen that made entertaining our family and friends much easier and more enjoyable.

In March we attended an assembly in Kristen's school where she received the Student of the Month Award and also the Math and Science Award. Later that week we returned to see her in a talent show given by her Brownie troop. After the show we went to her house for dinner. The award that Kristen received as the Student of the Month was a ten-dollar gift certificate for Borders' bookstore. I took her there and she chose two books for her ten dollars. The next week she asked me to take her back to Borders to buy some more books with her charge card. She was disappointed when she found out that the card was no longer usable.

Mike and I now had time to participate in community activities. Mike got carried away and became an officer of six organizations. He was president of the Board of Trustees at our church and at Center School. He was president of the Rotary

Club, secretary of the Twin Borough Scholarship Foundation, treasurer of the Washington Camp Ground Association and a member of the Board of Trustees of the National Museum of the American Revolution. He also volunteered to teach business courses to high school students in the Rotary "Bridging the Gap" program. As president of the Rotary Club he wrote a weekly newsletter each week as well as presided over the meetings. In preparation for the newsletter he interviewed a different member each week and wrote a brief biography of the member to be included in the newsletter. He had frequent meetings of the other organizations and kept busy at home working on their needs.

I was on two of the boards of organizations with him, Center School and the National Museum of the American Revolution. In addition to this I kept busy writing my book, giving dinners and playing with the grandchildren. I gave a speech at the Rotary Club in April and attended some of the meetings as Mike's guest. We visited a number of museums together to get ideas for our proposed museum. When we visited Cindy and Denis in April we looked at several museums with Cindy and Lucas while Denis was at work and Thomas was at school. In May we took a trip to Pinehurst, North Carolina to visit Mike's sister, Shirley, and her husband, Ed. On our way there we stopped for a few days at Virginia Beach where we visited several museums and on the way back we visited museums in Petersburg and Richmond, Virginia. We saw some interesting exhibits and brought back some good ideas for the proposed museum in New Jersey. While we were in Virginia we visited some of the houses where Mike had lived as a child. I enjoyed seeing Fort Monroe where he lived twice as a small child. He showed me his homes, church and school there and the ramparts where he and his friends had played. In Richmond we visited the house where he had lived when he was nine to eleven years old. The man who currently lived in the house was most gracious to us.

In the middle of May we enjoyed a delightful four days with the Deipnos at the Victorian Inn in Cape May that we had discovered back in December. Tom and Simi Long drove up from Georgia to be with us and it was a great reunion. The Deipnos have continued to meet every month during our retirement. Some of the authors that members of the group have selected during that time are: Jane Austin, Boccaccio, Daniel Boorstin, Cicero, Daniel Defoe, Nathaniel Hawthorne, Homer, Henry James and David McCullough. We meet on the first Saturday of each month and our discussions are as lively as ever. When our two newest members, Joan and Jim McCoy, heard about our history of special trips, they mentioned that they had never been on a cruise and would like to go on one. The group investigated a number of options and voted to go on a cruise on the Danube River the following spring.

At the end of May Mike and I traveled to a Rotary Convention in Philadelphia. The dinner was a black tie affair and Mike wore the tuxedo that his mother had bought him fifty years ago while he was in high school. It fit him perfectly and he looked very handsome. We danced the night away and had a wonderful time. June was a busy month for us. We hosted a dinner for some of our Bound Brook friends at the beginning of the month. Several of the guests had never been to our house and they enjoyed the dinner and the games afterwards.

Later in the month we drove to Rockport and opened the house for the summer. After we cleaned the house and painted the stairs, we took off for a three-day vacation in Maine. We found a charming inn on the ocean and stayed for two nights. A river flowed by our cabin into the harbor on which the inn was situated. I swam in the river, which was warmer than the ocean at Rockport at that time of the year. In the evening we ate at a charming restaurant and then watched a movie back in our cabin.

Each morning we had a complimentary breakfast, which we ate sitting on the porch of the inn overlooking the harbor. The inn offered a wide array of fresh fruit for breakfast, which was perfect for our diets. After breakfast we drove to York Beach for lunch and then up to Portsmouth. We visited old friends, Barbara and Bob Anderson, whom we had known in Bound Brook many years before. Barbara and I had been joint superintendents of our church school in Bound Brook and had worked well together. It was fun to see them again and they insisted that we stay for dinner.

The last day at the inn was not the most enjoyable for Mike. He threw his back out lifting a chair early in the morning. We visited a chiropractor and he was able to relieve some of Mike's pain, but I spent the rest of the day driving him around to see the lovely homes in York. We spent our last night eating at an elegant restaurant situated on a jetty overlooking the ocean. We drove back to Rockport the following morning and left for Bound Brook the next day.

We continued our plan to entertain the older grandchildren one at a time in Rockport. Sarah stayed with us the second week of July. She picked blueberries and made blueberry muffins and pancakes. We swam and read together and visited Bearskin Neck daily. She also enjoyed visiting my cousin Mimi at her house. On the 14th Mike took Sarah home and brought Cortlandt to Rockport. Mike and he climbed on the rocks and read books together and I took him to Bearskin Neck. Mike took him home at the end of his visit and returned to be with Cindy and her family the end of the month. Peter and Steve joined us with their families.

The big project for the summer was to install new windows in all the rooms of the Rockport house-35 windows in all. Mike, Denis, Steve and Peter tackled the job. Mike and Denis took out all the old rotted windows, Steve installed the new windows and Peter caulked them. Each man was well suited to his job, especially Peter, a perfectionist, who carefully caulked each window. When the job was finished it was a joy to raise and lower windows effortlessly and never have to find sticks to prop up windows anymore. I felt sorry for Dorianne who looked forward to relaxing in Rockport each year while Peter watched their energetic children. She never enjoyed that luxury, as every year there was a new project that Peter felt obligated to support.

On July 31st a terrible tragedy occurred. Jimmy Willing, the son of my cousin Bob, drowned. Bob Willing is our neighbor at Rockport; he and I each own a portion of the land my grandfather purchased in 1908. We walk through his yard whenever we go swimming off the rocks. Jimmy and his wife, Kelly, had come with their friends from the mid-west to visit the family in Rockport. They had been scuba diving off the rocks hoping to catch some lobsters for lunch. When I came down to the rocks to go swimming I saw them bucking the waves in the outer pool. The water was quite rough and Jimmy's friend had lost his weight belt. They came out of the water onto the rocks and I decided that the water looked too choppy for swimming. While I stood there with them Jimmy announced that he was going back to look for lobsters one more time. His wife advised him not to go, but he said that he had half a tank of oxygen left and he wouldn't be long. As he swam away she called after him to take her tank that was full, but he seemed not to hear her.

I went up to the house, changed my clothes and went food shopping. When I returned a police car turned onto Eden Road in front of me and then turned into our yard. I asked the officer why he was there and he said there was some trouble on the rocks. Just then the wife of Jimmy's friend came up to our house and asked to use our phone to call Bob Willing. She told us that Jimmy had been under the water for over an hour. After she made her call I called Bob back and gave him more details. He said that he would call Jimmy's cousin Andy McDowell to help find him as they frequently went diving together and he would know where to look. Bob said that he and his wife, Sally, would drive to Rockport immediately from Boston. I walked down to the rocks and found Kelly standing on a rock looking hopelessly at the ocean, which had developed big waves. I stood with my arm around her for almost an hour as we watched the harbor patrol search for her husband. Soon helicopters joined the search, then Andy and his son, Adam, arrived and swam out to where they usually dove. They located Jimmy's body and the harbor patrol pulled him up. Bob and Sally arrived shortly before they found the body. It was a horrifying experience.

The funeral service was held in the family church in Winchester the next day. All of our children were in Rockport at that time, so we all went to the service. Our children's spouses stayed with the grandchildren in Rockport while we traveled to Winchester. The church was overflowing with friends and relatives as Jimmy had grown up in Winchester. Bob and Sally hosted a reception in the church social hall after the service where we saw most of the relatives.

Early in August my brothers David and Bunkie visited us in Rockport with their wives. We talked, ate, reminisced and swam off the rocks together every day. After they left Kristen spent her week alone with us. We had a wonderful time together. We swam to the islands off of our rocks, went to the beach and to Bearskin Neck. Her favorite shop was The Country Store where she bought candy every day. She also liked to visit Mimi and Elizabeth and play *Trivial Pursuit* with Elizabeth and me.

Mike and I spent the third week of August in Lancaster where Mike helped Peter with his plumbing project and I helped Dorianne with the children at the pool. On Labor Day weekend Steve's family joined us at Rockport. We had a great time together. Steve cooked breakfast or supplied us with doughnuts and muffins every morning. When Mike left with Steve's family on Monday night I determined to begin the writing of this book. But before I started I visited Jimmy's wife, Kelly. She is a lovely woman and I enjoyed talking with her. Jimmy's sister, Patsy, took Kelly under her wing. They spent a great deal of time sitting on the rocks while Patsy's children played in the pools. Kelly is close in age to Patsy and spent the winter with her family in Winchester.

For two weeks at Rockport I immersed myself in my new passion, writing my book. I had brought with me all the journals that my grandmother had written and I began with my ancestral history. I wrote for twelve to fifteen hours a day and made a significant advance in the book's creation. I returned to Bound Brook to see Kristen in her school ceremony on the anniversary of September 11. Kristen had a speaking part and she and her classmates sang patriotic songs. She and her siblings were dressed in red, white and blue outfits and I took pictures of them. The next day Mike and I took Victoria and Nicole to Dunkin' Donuts and the park. We had dinner with Steve, Janice and the children that night. Then I returned to Rockport to continue working on my book for another week, while Mike caught up on his work in Bound Brook.

When Mike returned to Rockport we hosted a dinner for Uncle Bob, his children and their spouses, plus Mimi and Joe. During the past year we had been with Uncle Bob, Karen and Jon on several occasions and we enjoyed the opportunity to know them better. We prepared a sumptuous meal for them. Mike made a big fruit salad and I cooked the main course and the dessert. It was the first time that Karen, her husband, Sandy, Jon and his wife, Connie, had been to dinner at our house. The evening was delightful and Uncle Bob was fascinated to hear all about Florence Nightingale. He had asked me for a copy of my dissertation about her and also a copy of her biography that I had written as an introduction to the recently published edition of her *Notes on Nursing*. He seemed thrilled when I presented the books to him and he always mentioned them in future letters to me. He quizzed me about my work and we flattered each other on our careers. He was very modest about his authorship of the definitive textbook on pediatric anesthesiology that is now in its eighth edition. He is world renown yet humble about his fame.

Mike and I returned to Bound Brook on Sunday night and went to see Kristen's soccer game the next afternoon, followed by dinner at her house. On Wednesday night we sat for the children while Steve and Janice attended parents' night at Kristen's school. They came home with glowing reports on Kristen. I worked on my book at home for a week and then returned to Rockport with Mike to close the house for the winter.

In early October we flew to New Orleans for the wedding of Karen's daughter Ellen. We had a family reunion at the Hampton Inn where we stayed. My brothers David and Bunkie and their wives, Mary and Ann, were there as well as Mimi and Joe and their daughter, Elizabeth. We enjoyed socializing with them at the complimentary cocktail hours and breakfasts at the hotel. We were entertained royally at dinners and receptions hosted by the families of the bride and groom.

The morning of the wedding day David, Mary, Bunkie, Ann, Mike and I took the trolley into downtown New Orleans for some sightseeing. In the afternoon the wedding was held in the yard of an elegant mansion, followed by the reception inside the mansion. The food was plentiful and delicious and a band played our favorite jazz tunes. We ate, talked to our relatives and danced to the music. After the reception everyone was bused to a nightclub for more entertainment and socializing. We ended our stay the following morning with a fancy brunch held in another mansion near our hotel. It was a marvelous weekend and we enjoyed sharing it with our close relatives. But sadly it was the last time that we saw David's wife, Mary.

After we returned to Bound Brook Mike offered our house for a Rotary dinner. Forty people came for a buffet dinner before going to our local theater for a benefit affair. Mike made the fruit cup for the dinner and helped as much as he could as compensation for surprising me with the event. We received many compliments on the dinner and after it was over I felt good about it. After cleaning up I returned to my book for a few more days

At the beginning of November we began to include Brad in our routine of taking the twins to the park. Brad couldn't wait to get out the door when we picked them up at their house. We stopped at Dunkin Donuts for lunch and they enjoyed running up and down the restaurant while Mike ordered the food. Then we drove to Colonial Park where they climbed on the jungle gyms, played in the sand and walked along the path by the lake. There were physical fitness exercises at intervals along the path and they all liked trying to do pull-ups, sit-ups, push-ups and balancing exercises. We stayed at the park for about an hour each time and then stopped for ice-cream cones on the way back to their house. We look forward to our outings with the grandchildren each week.

20

Rough Sledding

In November 2002 I went for a routine physical examination to my family practitioner, Dr. Ryan. He sent me to Dr Stewart, a gynecologist, for an additional check up. Dr Steward ordered an ultrasound test; the result of the test showed a small tumor in my uterus that could be cancerous. Dr. Stewart recommended an oncologist at the cancer center in New Brunswick, New Jersey, but we could not get an appointment for six weeks. When we informed Peter of the situation, including the six-week delay, he immediately lined up an appointment for me with an oncology specialist in gynecology at Johns Hopkins Hospital. On December 9th we traveled to Baltimore and spent the night in a motel so that we could visit the specialist early the next morning. Dr. Whetmore told us that the ultrasound had been misread and he did not think that I had a tumor. He said that I had an old fibroid that was disintegrating but he doubted that I had cancer. We were very relieved. However the doctor did recommend that the uterus be scraped for analysis of the tissue to determine for certain whether any cancer was present.

We drove home and continued our regular routine. Mike bought a Christmas tree that Kristen helped me decorate and, on Sunday, Mike and I went to President Smith's Christmas party for Wagner

College. On Monday we drove back to the little motel in Baltimore and I had my uterus dilated and scraped the next morning at Johns Hopkins. Dr. Whetmore still believed that I did not have cancer and sent us home. The next day we drove to Lancaster as Dorianne was in labor with her fourth baby. It turned out to be false labor, but while we were at their house Dr. Whetmore called. He told me that the lab result from the uterine scraping showed that I had cancer in the lining of the uterus. He recommended a complete hysterectomy, but stated that there was no hurry to have the operation as my type of cancer grew very slowly in someone of my age. I told him that I wanted the operation as soon as possible, even if it had to be on Christmas Day. He agreed to perform the operation soon, but he said that he was only doing so to placate me because I was so worried.

Mike and I returned home, took the grandchildren to the park and had dinner at Steve's house. I had a Cat Scan on December 21st and we celebrated Christmas with the family at our house on December 26th. Dr. Whetmore's secretary called and told me that my operation was scheduled for December 31st. Dorianne delivered her baby on December 27th and we drove to Lancaster the same day to see our newest grandchild, Braden Beckford Schuyler. Peter had arranged for us to spend three nights at a resort hotel in Lancaster. Being in that lovely hotel and spending time with Pete and his family helped me get through those last few days before my surgery.

Mike and I had decided to spend the night in Baltimore at the Tremont Plaza, an inexpensive yet elegant hotel that we had visited several years before. It was an apartment building that had been converted to a hotel with suites of rooms. I had to spend the afternoon and evening drinking four liters of electrolyte fluid to clean out my intestinal tract completely. We knew that we would be stuck in the hotel so we decided to be as comfortable as possible. We had a suite with a hall, living room, dining room, kitchen, bedroom and bath. We bought meals for Mike in the hotel deli and I watched him eat at our dining room table. Between frequent trips to the bathroom I watched the movie, *Kindergarten Cop,* on the television with Mike. I also worked on my book as I was afraid that I might not survive the operation.

On the morning of December 31st I entered Johns Hopkins Hospital at 9:00 am for an 11:00 am operation. I brought along my notepad so that I could spend my last hours working on my book. However, the operation that was scheduled before mine was canceled, so I was whisked into the operating room and they did my operation early. Dr. Whetmore performed a total abdominal hysterectomy, a bilateral salpingo-oophorectomy and removed the surrounding lymph nodes. I responded so well to the operation that I was sent right to my room where Mike was waiting for me. He never left my side the entire time I was in the hospital. He slept in a reclining chair by my side and tied a string to his wrist and the side rail of my bed at night so I could get his attention if I needed him. Cindy traveled from Seattle to Baltimore the next day and also stayed with me every day. She spent the nights in a nearby motel.

On the first day after the operation I did not feel the pain as the epidural anesthetic was still in effect. But the next day was a day from Hell. The doctor had the epidural removed and I was in excruciating pain. Dr. Whetmore prescribed the drug, OxyContin, to alleviate the pain and it nearly killed me. My respiration dropped to six per minute, my speech was slurred and I couldn't open my eyes. Two nurses gave me a powerful antidote that could cause convulsions if not administrated carefully. It brought my breathing rate up temporarily, but then it wore off and I went back into a stupor. The nurses had to give me more of the antidote. That night I had nightmares and hallucinations like those depicted in Kafka's book, *The Trial.* The hallucinations continued the next day and the nurse advised me not to take any more OxyContin; I agreed with her completely.

That day Dr. Whetmore came into my room and advised me to continue taking OxyContin for pain even after I went home. The antidote, if needed, had to be given intravenously and he intended to send me home with an intravenous cut-down so that I could take the antidote if needed at home. I couldn't believe that he would suggest such a thing after what I had been through. I told him I would not take that drug ever again. Mike called my nurse into the room and asked her to work out a plan for my pain control with another drug. She conferred with a resident doctor and suggested 600 mg of Motrin every six hours with 600 mg of Tylenol in between to carry me over the lapse between dosages of Motrin. The plan worked and we were most grateful to my nurse, Tammy.

I also asked one of my nurses to remove the intravenous cut-downs still left in my hand, which she did. Someone from the blood work department came to my room two different times to insert another intravenous opening into my veins, but I refused to allow it both times. She threatened to report me to the doctor and I encouraged her to do so. She did not return to try again.

On January 4th I left Johns Hopkins and rode home with Cindy and Mike. We made a pit stop on Route 295 and Cindy helped me into the rest room. While we ate lunch in the restaurant we ran into a professor whom I knew from Wagner College. We arrived in Bound Brook late in the afternoon. Steve came over with Victoria and Kristen to see me. He hugged me for a long time with tears in his eyes. It was wonderful to be home again. The next day Cindy cleaned up the kitchen and did a load of laundry before leaving for the train with Steve. She took the train to Baltimore where she boarded the plane for her return trip to Seattle. Her visit was a godsend to me and I will always be grateful for her thoughtfulness.

After Cindy left Peter arrived with his children. While Mike took the grandchildren to the park, Peter spent two hours talking with me and it was great to spend so much time alone with him. That evening after Peter left, I called my close friends and relatives to tell them that I was at home and doing well. The pain from the operation continued, but the Motrin really helped alleviate it. Mike got up in the middle of the night when the medication wore off. He went down to the kitchen for milk, crackers and the pill and brought them up to me. He kept this up every night until the pain finally started to abate. He was always cheerful and very caring to me. I felt so grateful to have such a loving family.

On the second morning after I came home I lay in bed for over an hour talking to God. I thanked him for my life, my Mike, my children, their spouses, my grandchildren and all my friends. I felt calm and happy and not at all bitter about having cancer. Throughout my life I had been terrified of getting cancer, but now that I had it I accepted it and felt grateful that God had given me such a wonderful life and was still taking care of me.

Cathy and Carrie visited me the next day. They took the ornaments off of the Christmas tree and handed them to me to put back in the boxes. Flowers and cards started to arrive and friends called to see how I was. Nicole, Victoria and Brad came to visit me on Thursday and Beverly Weber brought us dinner on Friday. She continued to bring us dinner frequently for the next several months. Cards and flowers kept arriving, over 200 cards in all, and so many friends and relatives called me over the next few months.

Dr. Whetmore called to tell me the results of the pathological report. All the cancer had been removed and all of the lymph nodes were negative for cancer. The Tumor Board at Johns Hopkins, made up of ten doctors and one nurse, recommended giving me total pelvic radiation and four to six cycles of Taxol/

Platinum chemotherapy, plus Herceptin, to prevent any recurrence of cancer. Johns Hopkins was too far to travel for daily treatments so we investigated options for treatment in our area.

Beverly Weber is a personal friend of one of the top doctors at Hunterdon Medical Center, so I asked her to find out from him whom he would recommend for my radiation therapy. His wife, who is also a doctor, had received radiation under the care of Dr. Fein at the Cancer Center in Hunterdon Medical Center and she highly recommended him. I went to see Dr. Fein on January 14th in preparation for my radiation treatment. When he examined me I showed him my hysterectomy scar that was red and inflamed with a red circle next to it which was enlarging. He said it was an infection and prescribed the antibiotic, Keflex, which I was to take before starting the treatment.

I had an appointment with Dr. Whetmore in Baltimore the next day. I advised him about the infection in my incision and he told me not to worry, as it would go away. I mentioned the medicine that Dr. Fein had prescribed and he said to go ahead and take it if I thought it would help. He commented that doctors often prescribe antibiotics for psychological affect on patients when it really isn't necessary. During the trip home from Baltimore I was in severe pain. The infection and the pain did not get better during the week so I visited our family doctor for reassurance. He was gracious and caring, as I knew he would be. He thought the red circle might be a boil and he sent me to Dr. Stewart for his opinion. Dr. Stewart removed all the thick bandages that Dr. Whetmore had placed on my abdomen. He told me to expose the incision to the air, wash it regularly with soap and water and take a stronger antibiotic, Ceproflexin. The infection started to heal. When I returned to Dr. Stewart the next week the redness on the incision had subsided but the round spot next to it was still red.

I called Dr. Whetmore for his advice and he urged me to begin the radiation treatments immediately. He believed that the red circle was a stitch, which would soon be absorbed and disappear. I passed on these comments to Dr. Fein. Dr. Fein was hesitant to begin radiation, but he deferred to Dr. Whetmore's advice because of his prominent position at Johns Hopkins. On February 4th I began a six-week period of daily radiation treatments. Mike drove me to the Cancer Center every weekday and waited for me during my treatment. Soon after I started receiving radiation my incision began to get redder again. Mike drove me down to Baltimore for my final visit to Dr. Whetmore a week after the radiation treatment started. He took out the staples over the incision and I again asked him if it was infected. He again replied not to worry about it as it would go away. As the radiation treatments continued the redness spread. Dr. Fein was concerned and he renewed the antibiotic that Dr. Stewart had prescribed for ten more days.

While I was talking to Dr. Fein I mentioned that I had been to see his colleague, Dr. Quinn, the oncologist who would be managing my chemotherapy when I finished the radiation. I told Dr. Fein how impressed Mike and I were with Dr. Quinn's sincere interest in us. I related that he had treated us with great respect and talked to us as if we were intelligent people. Dr Fein gave me a wry grin and said, "Oh my, we'll have to do something about that."

During the radiation treatments I went on with my regular life. Mike and I took Nicole, Victoria and Brad to lunch and to the park once a week and Kristen came to church with us on Sundays. I went to the birthday parties of Victoria, Nicole and Brad in February—Peter's and Cathy's families were there also. Then we all drove to Carrie's party in Danbury on March 2nd. The next day I was admitted to Hunterdon Medical Center for a severe infection of my incision. The radiation had interfered with the healing process of my infection as it prevented my body from creating new cells to replace the infected ones. Dr. Fein referred me to Dr. Gugliatta, the leading infection specialist at the medical center. When Dr. Gugliatta examined my abdomen he immediately admitted me to the hospital that afternoon. He treated me with intravenous antibiotics for the next two weeks in the hospital, but he allowed the radiation treatments to be completed.

I was very impressed with Hunterdon Medical Center. The nurses on 5 North were excellent. My favorite nurse, Bett, was a true patient advocate and took marvelous care of me during my stay. Mike came to see me every morning, ate breakfast with me and stayed with me all day and evening. We watched movies together every evening on television and he left at 10:30 each night. A series of old Oscar-winning movies was being shown and we enjoyed watching them.

Dr. Gugliatta gave me a number of antibiotics intravenously. The one that seemed most effective was Vancomycin. However it was caustic and the nurses had to keep finding new veins in which to insert it. I had hoped to go home at the end of the first week as our Deipno meeting was scheduled for Saturday. However Dr. Gugliatta felt that I was not ready to be discharged. I was very disappointed, as I had never missed a Deipno meeting. The nurses were very sympathetic and offered to bring the Deipnos in through the emergency room and let us have our meeting in the visitors' room on the fifth floor. The hostess for the Deipno meeting had already prepared the meal so the plan did not work out, but I really appreciated the thoughtfulness of the staff.

The next day Steve and Janice brought their four children over to the hospital to cheer me up. They had colored pictures for me and we gathered in the visitors' room where we could socialize. We had the room to ourselves and when the door was shut no one could hear the children romping around the room. It was a wonderful visit and I was so grateful to Steve and Janice for bringing the children to see me. On Sunday their whole family went to the Ringling Brothers' Circus at the Meadowlands. That night they came to the hospital to visit me again. We watched a video of the circus on the television set in the visitors' room. The weekend turned out to be a happy experience after all.

On Monday a surgeon colleague of Dr. Gugliatta told me that he wanted to open up my incision to see if he could find what was causing the infection. I told him, "absolutely not!" I refused to have any more invasive surgery. That night some one came to my room and took blood and another person performed an electrocardiogram on me early the next morning. In the morning I informed my nurse, Bett, that I suspected there was a plan to perform surgery on me. Bett looked at my chart and noticed that my radiation treatment had been changed to the morning and that an operation room has been reserved for me at 3:00 p.m. Mike was planning to go to a Rotary luncheon, so I called him and caught him in time to tell him to come right to the hospital instead. By the time he arrived, Bett had called Dr. Gugliatta and requested that he cancel the surgery, which he did. Bett told me that she would not have let the orderlies take me to the operating room if they had come to get me.

That afternoon I had my last radiation treatment. The nurses gave me a diploma and they and Dr. Fein said good-by to me with a big hug. Steve, Janice and the children came for one more visit and brought me pretty little flowers and pictures that they had made for me. Their visits meant so much to me! I again asked Dr. Gugliatta to let me go home on the weekend. He finally agreed to let me out on Saturday afternoon. He gave me a new antibiotic that I could take orally, Avelox. I continued to take this drug for a month and a half. I also continued to apply warm compresses over my incision several times a day.

We left the hospital after lunch and arrived home just in time to attend the installation service of the new minister at our church. Cathy, Rick and Carrie also attended the ceremony and when the minister, Rod Church, saw Cathy sitting with us he came over to speak to her. She had met him in London in the 1980's when she and a church group traveled to England. Rod greeted her enthusiastically and they sang a little duet together before the ceremony began. Cathy participated in the installation when the visiting ministers joined in the laying on of hands on the new minister. We chatted with Cathy and Rick at the reception in the church social hall and then they drove back to Danbury. Mike and I went home and changed into formal clothes to attend a Rotary dinner dance that evening. The next day Kristen and I took a short walk and then we went to dinner at her house. It was great to be free again.

But tragedy occurred the following day. My sister-in-law Mary Smith died of Lupus. My brother David and I had been calling each other frequently as both Mary and I had been suffering through illnesses. Mike flew to Wyoming for Mary's funeral service. I was still applying warm compresses five times a day and taking a powerful antibiotic every day and did not feel up to the long trip. While Mike was gone Steve took me under his wing. I had dinner at his house after Mike left and Steve came to church with Kristen and me on Sunday morning. He brought me home to his house again for dinner Sunday night. On Monday Cathy and Carrie visited to keep me company until Mike returned home. Steve, Janice and their children shared dinner with us almost every night for the rest of March. Sometimes we went to their house, other times they came to our house or we took them out to a restaurant. They really kept up my morale. Janice even volunteered to give Cathy's birthday party at her house.

In April we used our airplane tickets to Seattle that we had been unable to use in December. Mike convinced me that staying with Cindy and Denis would be similar to being at home as I could continue with the hot soaks and take frequent naps. I had a restful week in Seattle and slept a good deal of the time. Cindy prepared delicious meals for us and we so enjoyed being with Thomas and Lucas for several days. We also had an opportunity to see our nieces Heather and Andrea, who live near Seattle. We watched a movie on the couch with Cindy and Denis each evening after the boys went to bed and we loved being with them again.

When we returned to New Jersey we visited Dr. Gugliatta and he prescribed Avelox for another month. Steve, Janice and their children joined us in church on Easter Sunday. By the end of April I felt up to taking the four grandchildren to Dunkin' Donuts and the park with Mike's help. Mike and I rode in Steve's van to Lancaster to attend Braden's christening on April 27th. We treated Steve, Janice and their children to a room at the motel. We ate dinner at a restaurant next door and the children were given balloons much to their delight. We enjoyed the complimentary breakfast buffet and let the children run around while we sipped our second cups of coffee. Braden's christening ceremony was impressive and, afterwards, we gathered at Peter and Dorianne's house for refreshments and conversation.

On April 30th I visited Dr. Gugliatta and he declared that my infection was completely healed. He took me off all medications and wished me well. I was eternally grateful to him for healing me. After leaving Dr. Gugliatta's office, I went to the main hospital and arranged to see the Director of Nursing of the hospital. When I was ushered into her office I explained who I was and my experience at Wagner College. I mentioned that I wanted to commend a nurse who worked on the fifth floor of the hospital. I told her that Bett had been an excellent patient advocate and a highly responsible, dedicated and caring nurse to me. She said that the hospital was giving awards to outstanding nurses the next week and that she would see that Bett received one of these awards.

With my infection cured, I was now in condition to receive my chemotherapy sessions. Before I started, however, we celebrated by taking Nicole, Victoria and Brad to the playground twice, attended Kristen's soccer games, shared several meals with Steve's family and hosted a luncheon at our house for our new minister to meet several members of the congregation. I also drove to Staten Island to have lunch with some of my friends from Wagner College and, on the day before I started chemotherapy, we celebrated our traditional Mothers' Day and two birthdays at Ellery's. Dorianne's mother was visiting her so we invited her along. Mike presented all the women with corsages and we enjoyed our usual festive celebration with games, gifts, a delicious dinner and a big sheet cake. Steve and Janice gave me a large television set for my gift.

My chemotherapy began the next day. I received the medicine intravenously for seven hours straight. First I was given Herceptin, then Benedril to prevent allergic reactions, then Carboplatin, then Taxol and, finally, Kytril to prevent nausea. Mike sat next to me all day long and it was wonderful to have his company. I had been very anxious about having chemotherapy, but it turned out to be almost an enjoyable occasion with Mike constantly at my side. He bought us lunch, which we ate together while the IV dripped and, later, he bought us good humors for an afternoon snack. We read books together and, after the Benedril, I fell asleep for a while. We were amazed to see how cheerful the other patients were during their treatments. Almost all of the patients had a relative or friend with them during their chemotherapy infusions and none of them seemed depressed.

I received four seven-hour treatments, each followed by a three-week rest period. I felt quite well between treatments. The entire process took three months. Mike drove me to the Cancer Center for treatments and stayed with me the whole seven hours each time. I lost all of my hair by the end of June so I wore a sun hat for the rest of the summer and fall. I continued to live my normal life during the three months of chemotherapy. We took Victoria, Nicole and Brad to Dunkin' Donuts and the park and frequently went to restaurants with our children and their families. Kristen's school concert was on the day of my second round of chemotherapy. We had hoped to attend the concert at 6:00 p.m. after my treatment. However the treatment continued until 6:45 p.m. so we didn't arrive at Weston School until the end of the concert. We saw Kristen sing in the last number and then we went to McDonald's with her and her family.

We took Kristen and her sisters to see the movie, *Finding Nemo*, which we all thoroughly enjoyed. I hosted a party for Steve's birthday at our house and the next day Janice had a party for him at their house. Unfortunately, at the end of the party, Kristen fell off her bike and broke her leg. She was very discouraged as it was the last week of school and she would miss participating in the parties and sports events at the end of the school year. She was also frustrated by the fact that she would not be able to swim all summer. Steve took her to the doctor the next day and he put a cast on her leg. I gave her a cuddly stuffed kitten and played cards with her and her sisters the following day. Kristen learned very quickly to walk with crutches and she was able to go back to school for the last two days of the semester. Her classmates signed her cast, which cheered her up.

When I went to the Cancer Center for my third treatment the blood test showed a decrease in my white blood cells. The doctor gave me the chemotherapy but told me to return the next day for an injection to stimulate my production of white blood cells. After the injection I thought that I could feel blood cells popping out of my bone marrow all night long and at the next blood test my white cells had quadrupled in number.

A few days later we heard that Denis' father had died of a heart attack. Mike and I drove down to Arlington, Virginia for his wake and Cathy came with us. Cathy, Mike and I took Thomas and Lucas back to the hotel after we had paid our respects to Denis and his family. It was nice to be able to spend some time with the boys as we saw them so infrequently.

At the beginning of July we visited Rockport for a week with Steve, Peter and Cathy and their families. We celebrated Kristen's and Malcolm's birthdays on July 3rd and Dorianne's relatives came down to join in the celebration. On July 4th I discovered a few sores on my abdomen and, after all my previous trouble with infection, we were concerned that I might be having a relapse. Mike took me to the emergency room of the hospital in Gloucester and the doctor diagnosed the sores as shingles. He gave me medicine, Famvir, to prevent the shingles from spreading and sent me home after a three-hour wait. That evening we all went to the holiday parade. The next day Mike and I drove to the North Shore Mall and bought a large wagon so that we could take Kristen for walks with her broken leg. We took her to Bearskin Neck in the wagon while the other grandchildren were at the beach; the wagon was also handy for our walks after dinner with the children.

Mike mentioned to Steve that he was considering buying a shed someday for Rockport, to put the big toys and tools in. Steve, in his typical fashion, immediately called up the lumber store and ordered supplies to build a shed. The next weekend he brought Ray Woldin and his wife, Barbara, to Rockport with him and Ray helped him construct a new shed in a day and a half. We all went back to Bound Brook at the end of the weekend.

July 14th was the day of my final chemotherapy treatment. Afterwards I spent several days playing with Kristen; then Mike and I traveled to Lancaster so Mike could help Peter again with the plumbing in his bathroom. When we returned to Bound Brook two of my best friends from Wagner College, Marilyn Kiss and Mildred Nelson, drove over from Staten Island and treated me to lunch at Applebee's restaurant. They had been so supportive during my illness and visited me several times.

I gave Mike a birthday party in Bound Brook and then we drove to Rockport where I spent the rest of the summer and swam every day. On August 9th relatives started to arrive. Our four children came and my three brothers also came with their families. The first event was a picnic at the Gordons' house and after that we entertained twenty to twenty-five relatives for dinner at our house every night for the next ten days. Each evening, a different relative bought and cooked the meal. On the 13th my brothers and I drove to Cambridge with our spouses for the internment of Mary's ashes. The minister who conducted the service was the minister at the Rockport Episcopal church and also knew Mary in Cody, Wyoming. It was a lovely service and the minister really captured Mary's personality. When we returned to Rockport Cindy had a delicious dinner waiting for us.

The project for the summer was a new roof for the house. The men again joined forces and managed to put the roof on in short order. Even my brother Bunkie joined the crew and claimed he enjoyed the roofing experience. Dorianne had to supervise her children again while Peter helped with the roof. We did cheer Dorianne some when we offered to baby-sit while she and Peter celebrated their 10th wedding anniversary at My Place, a picturesque restaurant by the sea. Dorianne looked gorgeous in her outfit and Peter's eyes were sparkling as he gazed at her in the car when they drove off.

On Sarah's ninth birthday we hosted a picnic for sixty guests. All the relatives from my side of the family, including the Gordons, and many of Dorianne's family came to the celebration. We put tables on the lawn, as Dorianne's mother

could not walk to the rocks. My children helped me prepare
the food and everyone seemed to have a good time. We captured
the enthusiasm of the guests in a number of great photographs.

The grandchildren had a wonderful time playing together during
their two weeks at Rockport. Kristen's cast precluded her from
going in the water and she was downcast whenever her cousins
went to the beach so I took her to the movies several times to
cheer her up. We saw the movie, *Freaky Friday,* and she liked
the music from the picture so much that she put on a show for
the relatives, singing the lead song on a toy microphone while
Nicole and Victoria accompanied her with a toy guitar and a
keyboard. I also took Kristen to see the Walt Disney movie,
Sinbad, which included episodes from Homer's *Odyssey* as well
as tales from the *Arabian Nights*. I taught her to play the adult
game, *Taboo*, and she became quite good at it. She and
Cortlandt enjoyed playing it together. David, Bunkie, Steve,
Janice and Peter paddled to Thatcher's Island in our kayaks
while they were there and I continued to swim. After everyone
went home, Mike and I took the linens to the Laundromat and
washed 38 towels and 20 sheets. My brothers and their families
stayed at local motels so that spared us from additional laundry.

Mike and I returned to Bound Brook and drove back to Rockport
four days later. I stayed on for another two weeks, worked on
my book and swam every day. Mike came up on weekends.
We went out to dinner with my Uncle Bob and his children the
evening before we closed the house for the winter. It had been
a marvelous celebration for me after finishing all my medical
treatments. A Cat Scan, taken in September, showed no evidence
of cancer anywhere.

In October Dorianne and Peter asked if we would take care of
Cortlandt and Malcolm for a weekend. We were delighted to
have them and we joined Steve, Janice and their children at the
Manville Community Fair on Saturday. The children enjoyed

the games and rides in the afternoon and the big fireworks display in the evening. On Sunday morning Kristen, Nicole, Victoria, Cortlandt and Malcolm joined us at church, then we all went to a restaurant for brunch.

At the end of the summer Mike and I felt that the older grandchildren were grown up enough to enjoy going on some special trips to New York City with us, and their parents agreed. I didn't feel quite strong enough to go into the city yet so Mike took Cortlandt and his best friend, Ian, on the first trip. The two boys spent the night at our house before the trip and they were excited. In the morning Mike took them to Liberty Park in Jersey City and then to the Statue of Liberty on the ferry. It was a rainy day but that didn't seem to bother them; they really enjoyed themselves and brought home souvenirs for their families. By October I felt stronger so we invited Sarah and Kristen to visit the Museum of Natural History in New York City with us. We drove in and parked under the museum. We saw the Hayden Planetarium presentation, the display of large animals of North America and Africa, an IMAX movie about the Asian tiger and a display of butterflies in a herbarium. The girls enjoyed watching a big butterfly sitting on top of a man's head, which he was unaware of. Of course their favorite spot in the museum was the gift shop. They not only bought souvenirs for themselves but toys for their younger siblings. We ate lunch in the museum cafeteria and came home with many wonderful memories.

That fall, Mike and I agreed to become mentors for two young boys at the local elementary school. Mentoring is a program of the local Rotary Club that Mike instituted when he was president of the club. Individual Rotarians meet with youngsters at the local school—typically children of single parents or from broken homes—who could benefit from extra adult attention and concern. Each mentor meets with his or her child once a week for about an hour. Mike and I meet with our students every Wednesday for an hour and thoroughly enjoy the experience. We each work individually with our own boy for the first part of the hour and then all four of us join together and play a game at the end of the hour.

Mike and I suggested to our students that they write books about themselves. Each week we brought in an outline to help them write about different aspects of their lives. We gave them disposable cameras to take pictures of their families, homes and classmates to illustrate the chapters that they wrote. The boys are quite different but they seem to enjoy playing games together. Mike's student is quiet, but after much questioning, Mike found that he was interested in snakes. They worked on a booklet about snakes together. My student is an avid soccer player and his team won a trophy. He likes most sports and I have developed an interest in the sports pages of the newspapers for the first time in my life. I clipped articles about his favorite teams from the newspaper all year and he put them together in another booklet about sports.

At the end of October the grandchildren dressed in costumes for Halloween. We added the extra page of *Tidings* to the "Kinformation" section showing pictures of all the grandchildren in their costumes. Thomas and Cortlandt dressed up as Harry Potter, Sarah was Hermione, Lucas was Spiderman, Brad was a lion, and Braden was a pumpkin. Kristen dressed up as Juliet, Victoria was Sleeping Beauty, Nicole was Jasmine and Carrie was a house. Malcolm refused to have anything to do with Halloween. He would not put on a costume and he shut the door on the children who came to his house for trick or treat.

Since we moved to the Bound Brook area in 1956, the local Congregational Church has played an important role in our lives. Almost every year Mike or I or both of us have served as an officer of the church or as a member of one of the church boards. In May 2001 I was elected as Church Clerk and have continued in that office since then. In November 2003, I attended an all day retreat for the officers of our church. It was a well-run retreat and I especially enjoyed the games that our minister had us play to get better acquainted. I found it a rewarding experience.

Shortly thereafter we went to Lancaster so Mike could help Peter with some more work in his bathroom. Dorianne was not sure that Peter would ever finish the task of renovating the main bathroom in their house. The family had been using a tiny bathroom in the basement, but the children were afraid to go down to the basement alone. So Dorianne was kept busy taking them to the bathroom as well as performing all the other tasks a mother of four small children has to do. Before we left we bought them a new bathtub and toilet. Peter was very appreciative, but it took Dorianne's brother-in-law, Arnie, to convince Peter to install them before he put in the new floor so that the family would have another bathroom to use while the renovation was being completed.

In mid-November Peter's high school classmates held their 25th reunion. He and Dorianne visited us for this occasion and we sat with Malcolm and Braden during the celebration. We were delighted to have the little boys and Dorianne and Peter had a grand time at the reunion. They spent the night at our house and the next morning we treated them and Steve's family to brunch at our favorite restaurant in South Bound Brook. Malcolm and Brad entertained us by having a sword fight with two spoons. The children were excited to be with each other and we had a great time.

Mike and I flew to Seattle on December 18th for an early Christmas with Cindy, Denis and the boys. As usual Cindy fed us well and we loved being with them. Our niece Andrea came for lunch on our last day there. On our return, we arrived in

New Jersey in the wee hours of the morning of December 24th. Mike and Steve found us a tree that morning and Kristen, Victoria and Nicole helped me trim it in the afternoon. We met Steve's family at our church at 8:00 p.m. for the Christmas Eve service. On Christmas Day Janice invited us to a turkey dinner. Her brother John, his girlfriend, Heidi, and Peter's family also came. Peter and his family spent the night at our house and in the morning Steve's family joined us for brunch. Cathy, Rick, Carrie, Mary and Julie arrived later and we all shared in opening gifts. We ended the day with the traditional roast beef dinner.

At the beginning of 2004 Mike came down with a severe case of pneumonia. He had not been feeling well for the three preceding days, but refused to go to the doctor. Before he was taken to the hospital in an ambulance on Tuesday evening, he had followed an exhausting schedule. On Saturday he got up early and drove to Princeton to obtain tickets to hear Toni Morrison as part of his fiftieth reunion program. He brought the tickets back home and gave them to Marilyn Kiss and Mildred Nelson to use, as we could not attend her talk. We ate lunch and then went to Brad's third birthday party while Marilyn and Mildred drove to Princeton to hear Morrison. We had a great time at Brad's party and left at 6:30 to dress in costumes for a masquerade ball given by the Rotary Club. Mike suggested that we leave the ball at 10:30, which was very unusual for him. He said that he felt very tired.

On Sunday I suggested that he make an appointment to see Dr. Ryan the next day. However, he said he was fine and went to pick up Victoria and Nicole for church and lunch afterwards. Sunday night he looked worn out and I told him he should go to bed. But he insisted that he must go to the Washington Camp Ground Association meeting where he was to give a report. He had lost his voice at that point, so he typed his report for someone else to read. After he left for his meeting I went to a meeting at our church. After my meeting was over I drove over to Mike's meeting. He looked haggard and could hardly walk to his car. I insisted that he go to see Dr. Ryan in the morning, but when he awoke he said he felt fine and wanted to drive to the Jersey shore to take a widowed friend of ours to lunch. We enjoyed the lunch and went back to her house for dessert and conversation. When we returned to Bound Brook he said he wanted to go square dancing and promised to take it easy and not dance every dance. I gave in as usual and hoped he was really getting better.

On Tuesday he insisted on going to the Rotary luncheon meeting, but when he came home he decided to take a nap. He slept all afternoon and when he woke up at 6:00 o'clock he was too weak to get out of bed. I took his temperature and it was 101 degrees. He lay in bed for a while and then staggered downstairs to watch television from the couch. A little later I looked at him and his face was bright red. I took his temperature again and it was 105 degrees. I called Dr. Ryan and he told me to take him to the hospital. I told him that Mike couldn't stand up so he said, "call 911 and get an ambulance." When Mike arrived at the emergency ward he was given antibiotics intravenously and by 2:00 a m, when he was admitted to a hospital room, his temperature had dropped. The x-ray showed that his right lung was full of pneumonia.

Mike stayed in the hospital for a week and I stayed with him every day from morning to midnight overseeing his care. I was happy to have a chance to care for him even though I could never return all the love and support that he had given me over the last year. Our family doctor, Dr. Ryan, and the lung specialist, Dr. Iorio, provided excellent care. They called each morning to check on Mike's progress and visited him in person every day. Dr. Ryan came in the late afternoon and always sat and talked with us for fifteen minutes or more. Dr. Iorio came at 11:30 p.m. and did the same thing. Dr. Iorio reminded us of Dr. Gugliatta, my infection specialist. They looked somewhat alike and they both worked late in the evenings. They were highly respected specialists but came to visit in casual clothes and were very empathic toward their patients. Mike and I felt extremely fortunate to have such dedicated, personable and intelligent doctors. Dr. Ryan is the best family doctor that we have ever had. On the morning that Mike was to be discharged from the hospital I had another Cat Scan done at Hunterdon Medical Center and then went to his hospital to drive him home. I again found out that there was no cancer anywhere in my body. How relieved we both were to be healthy again.

21

Golden Anniversary

With the exception of Mike's pneumonia experience, the first half of 2004 turned out to be an exciting and enjoyable time. We resumed our schedule of taking Victoria, Nicole and Kristen to church each Sunday followed by lunch with Ralph Pritchard at Eddie's Café in South Bound Brook. We returned to our regular attendance at square dancing and began to go to the movies frequently. We joined a program at our church called *Alpha,* a religious discussion series that met Sunday evenings for ten weeks. Each Sunday we were served a meal, which was followed by the showing of a film about a religious topic. After seeing the videotape we met in small groups in different rooms to discuss the topic presented. Forty people signed up for the course and were divided into groups of eight. Each group ate dinner together and held a discussion after viewing the videotape. We met new people and had many enlightening discussions with them.

Mike and I continued to mentor our two boys at Smalley School and to take the grandchildren to the park each week. We joined Steve's family for dinner frequently and I continued to work on my book. At the end of January Mike and I flew to Daytona Beach in Florida for a short vacation. We stayed in a small motel on the ocean and ate at several charming restaurants. We visited several state parks including Clearwater Springs where we saw the manatees that Steve had told us so much about. When we returned to New Jersey I resumed my swimming at the YMCA each week.

In February Steve took his family to Disney World for a vacation. They spent five full days seeing many Disney figures, swimming in pools and riding on water slides. They came back bubbling with tales of their adventures. Mike and I met them at the airport and we had dinner at McDonald's on the way home where we heard marvelous stories of what it was like to try and see everything with four excited small children. They took great pictures of the children standing next to their favorite Disney characters, and I was thrilled when Janice presented me with copies of all of them for my albums. We celebrated the birthdays of Nicole, Victoria and Brad toward the end of February.

In March we traveled to visit the families of Peter and Cathy. We also visited our friend Mary Parenteau in the hospital where she was scheduled to have surgery for a tumor in her intestines. Luckily the doctor was able to remove all the cancer and she needed no further treatment. She seemed in good spirits on my visits to her after the operation.

Kristen asked me if she could interview me in order to write a biography of me for her class project. I was pleased to consent and answered all her questions. She received an "A" on her biography. She and her classmates invited the subjects of their biographies to their class to receive awards. Each student introduced her subject to the class and told what was the most surprising fact about him or her. Kristen told the class that her Nana did not have TV when she was a child. Her classmates were incredulous when they heard this. The students gave their subjects pretty flowers that they had made and a blue ribbon award.

Early in April my brother Steve and his wife, Carol, invited us to visit them in their new time-share apartment in Florida. The apartment building was on the ocean on an island next to Palm Beach. They had a double apartment with a connecting door so we had complete privacy. We celebrated Passover with them the first night we were there and Carol explained what the different foods symbolized. We ate our meals with them in the dining room of their apartment and had some great discussions together. The ocean was warm enough for swimming, which I did every day that I was there. Steve and Carol took us on a boat ride down the inland waterway to see all the mansions in Palm Beach. Carol urged us to go dancing after they went to bed, so we found a nice motel a block away with rooftop dancing until midnight. The view was so beautiful from the restaurant that we invited Steve, Carol and Michael to dinner there on our last night in Florida. We thoroughly enjoyed our visit with Steve and his family.

Another big event in April was Cathy's 40th birthday. She gave herself a big party at her house in Danbury. She had lots of projects for the children and some very original games for the adults to play. She served a delicious dinner and the desserts were plentiful and yummy. Steve and Janice's family attended. Steve drove us to Danbury in his van and we all had a great time.

We drove to Wagner College on April 21st to see the play *Bye Bye Birdie* on opening night. It was excellent. The following week I returned to Wagner to have lunch in the faculty dining room with my old "lunch gang," Mildred Nelson, Julie Barchitta, and Ammini Moorthy. Our table was near the door so as faculty came into the room they saw us and joined us at our table. We had a good time chatting together. After lunch Julie took us to the President's office to see Richard Guarasci. He was very gracious and we talked for twenty minutes. He seemed interested in my book as he had urged me in the past to write about our book group.

A few days later Mike and I traveled to Lancaster to see Sarah in her school talent show. She and her friend sang a duet and we were impressed with their singing. We took Sarah and her friend, plus their families, to Friendly's restaurant for ice cream after the show. A few days later we joined Cathy and Rick at the Mid-Hudson Civic Center in Poughkeepsie, New York to see Julie dance. The concert featured a 50-piece orchestra and a chorus of several hundred people. While the orchestra played and the chorus sang in front of the stage, ballet dancers performed on the stage. Julie was in the top-level group that danced in most of the numbers during the hour and a half program. Her dancing was first-rate and she looked beautiful. We were very proud and impressed with her performance. After the show we all met at Friendly's for ice cream.

The following week we joined the Deipnos for a cruise up the Danube River through Hungary, Austria and Germany. We flew out of Newark airport on Friday night arriving in Frankfurt at 6 a.m. We had a six-hour layover there, where we sat in the terminal blear-eyed from lack of sleep, and we finally boarded a plane for the last leg of the trip into Budapest. We arrived at our cruise ship, the Viking Pride, at 4 p.m. where I took a nap and Mike toured Budapest on foot for an hour.

The Viking Pride was a small ship with room for 130 passengers and a crew of 40. The passengers' rooms were large and comfortable with full windows on the outside of the ship. The dining and lounge rooms were charming with floor to ceiling windows on both sides so that we could always look out at the beautiful scenery along the Danube. In the dining room we found a table that could seat our whole group so that we could share our experiences each day. The food was ample and delicious and the service was exemplary. Every evening there was entertainment in the lounge and a bedtime snack was provided. Mike and I always ended the evening by dancing to the music of Miroslav, the ship's piano player. Miro (his nickname) was most accommodating and played our favorite waltzes and swing music.

Each morning we started the day with a generous breakfast buffet in the dining room. After breakfast there was usually a shore excursion. The first morning we toured Budapest by bus. The driver took us by the magnificent parliament buildings in Pest and across the bridge to Buda to see the hilltop castle complex and St. Mathias church with its glistening spire. We ate lunch on the ship and spent the afternoon looking at the picturesque scenery as we cruised along the Danube listening to Miro's music. Sweets and coffee were provided at four o'clock each afternoon in the lounge. That night we were received in the lounge by the captain and his crew and then treated to a splendid welcome dinner.

On Monday we docked in Vienna where our guide narrated a bus tour of the Ringstrasse which included awesome churches, palatial homes, parliament buildings, the opera house and the magnificent St Stephen's Cathedral, built in the Middle Ages. Our group enjoyed an Austrian meal for dinner and then gathered to discuss a book about Hungary. After our discussion Hungarian goulash was served for the evening snack—how appropriate.

One of the highlights of the cruise was the visit to Melk Abbey, a 900-year-old monastery perched on a promontory high above the river. Melk is one of the finest examples of the late German baroque period. Our favorite part of the abbey was the library with its cherub filled ceiling and its vast collection of volumes. The interior of the church was awesome with its orange marble pillars, gleaming golden carved pulpit and glorious ceiling frescoes. We returned to the ship at noon and enjoyed the bucolic scenery as we cruised up the Danube during lunch and the afternoon. After dinner the ship docked in Linz and our group walked into town. The shops were closed, but we looked at the beautiful exteriors of several churches. In the town-square was an interesting monument celebrating the end of the plague centuries ago.

The ship cruised during the night and when we awoke on Wednesday morning we were delighted to see the picturesque town of Passau outside of our window. Mike and I strolled into town for coffee in an outdoor cafe and then enjoyed an organ concert in St. Stephen's Cathedral at noon, where we listened to one of the world's largest pipe organs. It was a thrilling experience and, while we listened, we gazed at the ornate frescoes on the ceiling. The cathedral was built in the seventeenth century and was a superb example of the baroque style. For lunch we found a delightful outdoor restaurant surrounded by an array of brightly colored flowers with a view of a large castle on the opposite side of the river. After lunch we visited two toy stores and bought eleven little gifts for the grandchildren.

The theme for dinner that night was a seaman's meal. The waiters were dressed as sailors and they were in fine spirits in expectation of the talent show that they were going to perform for the passengers after dinner. The show was delightful, with the crew singing songs from their home countries and doing skits. Our waiter dressed up as Mozart and gave a hilarious impersonation of the musical genius. The audience applauded with glee at their antics.

When the ship docked at the medieval town of Regensburg, Mike and I strolled along the river and took pictures of Germany's oldest stone bridge, built in the twelfth century. In the center of town stood St. Peter's Gothic cathedral with its towering spires and beautiful stained glass windows. We wandered around the town and found the old town-hall and another toy store with fascinating hand made toys. On the way back to the ship we stopped at a pottery shop and bought a hand painted mug, the only souvenir that we bought on the whole trip.

That afternoon we took an excursion boat to one of Germany's oldest monasteries, Weltenburg Abbey, set on a bend in the river with stunning scenery on all sides. What I liked best about the abbey was the statue of St. George flood-lighted on the altar. He was sitting on his horse with a dragon on one side and the king's daughter on the other. The frescoes on the ceiling were stunning and we were told that the church is considered to be a masterpiece of high baroque in southern Germany.

We returned to the ship for dinner and an evening of folk music in the lounge. A local musician and comedian had been brought on board to entertain us. He played and sang delightful Bavarian tunes and involved the passengers in the show. He put funny hats on people in the audience and pulled them up on the stage to play unique musical instruments such as washboards and odd horns and symbols. We took some great pictures of Mike in a funny hat banging a washboard with a big spoon.

We toured Nuremberg on the last day of the trip. The bus took us to the grounds where the Nazi rallies were held and to the site of the war trials. The tour ended at the Christmas market, which is one of the oldest and most famous of Europe's markets. It was one of the most delightful places that we visited on the trip. There were colorful stalls with fresh vegetables and flowers and a band in bright red costumes playing exhilarating German songs. Mike and I sat on one of the benches in front of the bandstand sipping our drinks and listening to that wonderful music.

Our last evening was very festive. We enjoyed a sumptuous seven-course farewell dinner followed by entertainment in the lounge. After the show Mike and I ended our last evening dancing to Miro's music. The next morning we were driven to the airport to fly home. It had been a very relaxing and enjoyable week and it was fascinating to see the cathedrals we had read about in college art courses years before.

Our dear friend Bruce McCreary died while we were on the Danube cruise. On his deathbed he had requested that Beverly Weber and Mike Schuyler speak at his memorial service. Beverly spoke of his faithfulness to his family and to his civic activities, especially the many years that he had spent overseeing the original building of the Middlesex Library and the recent addition to it. In his eulogy, Mike placed Bruce among the few people who had enhanced his opinion of mankind. Mike commented, "(Bruce's) thoughtfulness, kindness, gentleness and integrity have served as models of human conduct." He told of Bruce's participation in the Deipnos and gave examples of his wide range of book selections. He told of Bruce's ability to consistently follow ethical and moral principles. Mike commented, "Today in our complex society . . . we have many focuses—our family, our careers, our social contacts, our vocations—and we respond to the many standards they impose. Bruce suffered from none of this turmoil. He had one focus—his love for Marion and for their children—and one standard—his deep religious faith . . . that guided him through all his activities." Mike mentioned that as a business associate of Bruce he gained an even greater respect for his honesty and probity. "In making business decisions, Bruce automatically followed the only road he considered, that of the most ethical behavior."

Mike concluded, "My friendship with Bruce is one of the deepest and most rewarding experiences of my life. He has been, and will continue to be, an inspiration to me." I was deeply moved by Mike's eulogy and agreed with him completely that Bruce was one of the finest people we had ever known. We had now lost two of the couples who were original and devoted members of the Deipnosophistical Society—John and Millie Sheehan and Marion and Bruce McCreary. They are sorely missed.

When we returned from Europe we resumed involvement in our regular activities—visits with the family, church, square dancing, mentoring, writing my book, issuing *Tidings* and even weeding the garden. On the last weekend in May Cindy and Denis flew to New Jersey to join us at reunions at Princeton University. Cindy celebrated her 25th reunion and Mike celebrated his 50th. It turned out to be an exciting weekend. We drove down to Princeton on Friday afternoon for class pictures, receptions and formal class dinners. Each class member wore a special sports jacket made out of material with a Princeton motif on it. Cindy's class jacket was cream colored with a black and orange design of tigers all over it. The lining of the jacket was made of material with names of all of her classmates printed on it. Mike's jacket was solid peach colored with a Princeton emblem on the pocket. His class won the prize for the highest attendance at a reunion.

After the class picture was taken Mike's class sat down to a formal dinner under a huge tent. We were served a delicious steak dinner. During dinner the Tigertone singing group entertained us with the old Princeton songs, which we knew by heart from college days. We joined in with great gusto and, after listening to a few short speeches, we adjourned to an adjacent courtyard for dancing under another big tent. We danced all evening to the music of Stan Rubin's band, the same music that we had danced to fifty years before. We drove back to Bound Brook at 1 a.m.

On Saturday we returned to Princeton for more celebrating. All the classes marched in the traditional "P-rade" in the afternoon. Mike's class was an amazing sight to behold—350 men in matching peach jackets coming down the road like a stream of peaches. When the "P-rade" was over we invited Cindy and Denis to Cloister Inn, Mike's eating club, where there was a reception with a great choice of delectable hors d'oeuvres. We enjoyed the food and the discussion with Cindy and Denis for about an hour while we rested our feet. We went back to the class tent where we were served a prime rib dinner. Then we were treated to a jazz concert by one of Mike's classmates. We visited other class reunions and danced to the music in their tents. We returned home at 1 a.m. again and fell into bed. It was a great reunion!

On Sunday we took Cindy, Denis and Steve's children to church and joined Ralph Pritchard for lunch in our little café in South Bound Brook. At three o'clock we met with all our children for a late Mothers' Day celebration. Cindy and Denis stayed an extra day so that they could attend this annual celebration for the first time. The party was on the second floor of Ellery's restaurant and, as usual, everyone had a great time. We drove Cindy and Denis to the airport the next day and came home for a long nap.

The next two weeks were filled with school programs and special family occasions. I visited Kristen's school to see a program given by her Gifted and Talented group. Then I attended the graduations of Victoria and Nicole from their pre-school and of Brad from his pre-school. The children were adorable in their presentations. The little ones sang lots of songs and they knew all the words and gestures for each song. Nana was very proud of them.

We hosted a party at our house on June 8th for Steve's birthday. Cathy, Rick and Carrie came down from Danbury to help us celebrate. Rick grilled the steak while Steve opened his gifts on the deck. He received two unique Frisbees and the children had a great time throwing them and chasing them around the yard. I found a perfect gift for Steve earlier in the month when I talked with his cousin Heidi on the phone. She informed me that her husband, Russell, had just published a book of his underwater photos. Knowing how much Steve enjoys underwater pictures, I asked Heidi to send us two copies in time for Steve's party. Russell sent us two autographed copies and Steve was thrilled with the gift. On June 12th Steve and

Janice went out to dinner and a movie to celebrate their tenth wedding anniversary while Mike and I sat with the four children.

Cindy and Denis flew back to New Jersey with their boys on June 16th to help prepare for the fiftieth wedding anniversary party that the children were giving us. There were festivities every evening before the party on Saturday. Steve and his family brought flowers and cards to us on the evening that Cindy and Denis arrived, as that was the actual anniversary date of our wedding. Thomas, Lucas and Steve's children were so excited to see each other that they ran round and round the house squealing with glee. Thursday evening we took both families to Burger King for dinner so that the children could play on the jungle gym while the adults ate their meals and talked together. The children had a great time and so did the adults. On Friday Bunkie and Ann arrived from Kansas and Janice hosted a dinner party to celebrate Bunkie's birthday. After dinner the children watched town fireworks from Steve's deck.

Saturday was the big day for our anniversary party. Cathy had arranged for a photographer to come to our house in the afternoon to photograph the whole family, all 23 of us. The party began at 5:30 p.m. and it was fantastic! Sixty-eight people attended and we enjoyed being with all of them. The music ensemble that entertained us all evening was a couple who had played dance music at Patullo's restaurant for many years. We used to dance to Art and Willie's music every Saturday evening at Patullo's. They had retired, but when I called them to play at our party they immediately agreed. I sent them a long list of our favorite songs and they played every one of them. They even played the grandchildren's favorite song, *Take Me Out to the Ball Game*. Mike and I danced to waltzes and swing tunes all evening. After gazing at us as we waltzed to the first tune, the grandchildren joined us on the dance floor and had a great time.

For the event Cindy and Denis created a video presentation entitled, *Connie and Mike—A Walk Through 50 Years*. It showed pictures of both of us throughout our lives. The photos were orchestrated with our favorite romantic songs while Cindy narrated the presentation. Mike and I were thrilled with the video and Denis copied it onto our computer so we could look at it over and over again. The children and several of the guests took pictures and we bought a special album to put all the pictures in so we could remember the most wonderful party that we had ever had.

Beverly Weber donated a gorgeous floral arrangement for our table and had a beautiful three-tiered cake made for the occasion. We received a number of stunning floral arrangements at home from relatives and friends. On the actual date of our anniversary Mike gave me a magnificent arrangement of yellow roses and other flowers. I put it in the middle of the dining room table on a golden tablecloth and we enjoyed it for the next week. Denis and Ann took photos of me next to it so I would always remember it. We hosted a brunch for all the relatives the day after the party to celebrate Father's Day and the birthdays of Denis and Cortlandt. There was a lot to eat and we talked and enjoyed each other's stories. We ended the day by ordering four large pizzas to eat on the deck while the children continued to play on our swings and the neighbors' jungle gym. The festivities lasted until late in the evening and after everyone had gone we brought in the food and went to bed.

What a magnificent celebration our children gave us for 50 years of marriage. We continually thank God for giving us such a special family. We are grateful for the four marvelous children that we have and all the delightful grandchildren that they have brought into the world. Each of our children married a spouse whom we greatly admire, and our children and their spouses are terrific parents. Our grandchildren are the joy of our lives and we adore each and every one of them.

Mike has been the most wonderful husband that I could ever have wished for. He is loving, patient, thoughtful, interesting and fun to be with. He is honorable, responsible, wise and stimulating. He is a true gentleman in every sense of the word. I have never met another man as perfect as he is and I am so grateful to God that we found each other when we were so young. I feel I'm the luckiest woman in the world.

Mike and I also appreciate the parents and grandparents that we were so fortunate to have. We are both grateful for the principles of love, honesty, responsibility, seeing good in others and forgiveness that they taught us, and for the love that they surrounded us with.

Writing this book has been a fantastic endeavor for me and it has brought back marvelous memories.

My father, Lyman, seated, flanked by his parents, circa 1929
Back row, left to right: Francis Jr., Janet, Robert, Marion

Four generations, 1937
My mother, standing; my great-
grandmother Cad, left: Me:
my grandmother Jane

Mike's parents, 1949
Wynona and Cortlandt Schuyler

My family at Rockport, 1948
Mother, Steve, Father, Me, Bunkie, David

Me, at age two

Mike with sister, Shirley, 1934

Mike, age four

Mike and Me at
high school dance, 1948

Me at Radcliffe, 1949

Mike and Me at Princeton, 1950

Summer in Paris with Mike's parents, 1952

Me at Columbia, 1954

Mike's graduation photo,
Princeton, 1954

Our wedding, June 16, 1954,
Winchester, Massachusetts

Our first two children, Cindy and Steve

Cathy, Peter, Cindy, Steve, 1964

1967. Back row: Mike, Me, Biodun
Children (l. to r.): Cindy, Peter, Cathy, Steve

Square Dance Outfits
Philippines, 1970

Gift of Kulingtang, Philippines, 1970
Back row: Rads, Mely & Amelita Guevara, Me, Mike
Front row: Peter, Cathy

Lebanon, 1970. Visit to Joseph Own (far left), whom
we sponsored through Save the Children Federation
Joseph's father and brother, George, are on right.

Our children on trip to
London, 1970

Cindy in Bangkok, 1970

Bicycle trip with Jack
and Ella Handen, 1973

Dinner at our home with Deipnos and friends, 1968
Left to right: Beverly Weber, John Sheehan, Richard Bower, Simi Long, Mike, Me
Marion McCreary, Dick Weber, Helen Ann Bower, Bruce McCreary

Cruise with Deipnos to celebrate 100th book, 1973
Adults (l. to r.): John Sheehan, Mildred Moore, Bruce and Marion McCreary, Mike and Me,
Dick and Beverly Weber, Simi and Tom Long. Children
(l. to r.): Amy McCreacy, Cathy and Peter Schuyler

The new Dr. Schuyler, 1975   Trip to England with Beverly and Dick Weber, 1975
                                     Horace Callis, Dick, Beverly, Me, Elsie Callis

Steve's graduation from Tampa University, 1979   Cindy's graduation from Princeton, 1979

Our 25th Wedding Anniversary, June 16, 1979

My parents' 50 Wedding Anniversary, June 25, 1979
Sarah, Heidi, Ralph, Steve Smith, Carol, Bunkie, Heather, Ann, Stephanie, Mike, Nancy, Cathy, Donna, Mary.
Middle, left side: Becky, Marion, Andrea, Jamie. Middle, right side: Me, Cindy, David.
Front: Peter, Father, Mother, Steve Schuyler

We purchase the Rockport house, 1981   Mike in front of new office, 1984

"Hammering Crew" for Wagner awards, 2000   Wagner College Commencement, 2001
Me, Marilyn Kiss, Sheryl Von Rolleston,   Mildred Nelson, President Smith, Me
Linda Raths, Julie Barchitta

Cindy and Dennis - October 4, 1992

Dorianne and Peter - August 14, 1993

Janice and Steve - June 12, 1994

Rick and Cathy - April 21, 1995

Cindy, Steve, Cathy, Peter at Peter's Wedding - August, 1993

Family picnic at Rockport - Summer, 1996
Back: Cathy, Rick, Mike, Steve.   Front: Julie, Elizabeth
Middle: Dennis, Cindy, Thomas, Me, Peter, Dorianne, Sarah, Mary, Janice,
Kristen, Janet & Frank Barnes

Clockwise from left: Denis, Cindy
Thomas, Lucas - 2003

Clockwise from lower left: Cortlandt, Sarah,
Braden, Dorianne, Peter, Malcolm - 2003

Julie, Carrie and Mary - 2003

Steve and Janice's Family - 2003
Back: Nicole, Kristen, Brad. Front: Victoria

Mike and Me on Alaskan Cruise, 1994

Mike in Istanbul, 1999

Mike and Me in Athens, 1999

Deipnos at Cape May, New Jersey, 2002
Back row: Me, Bruce, Beverly, Mildred, Lysle
Front row: Dick, Mike, Artie

July 4th parade in Rockport, 1999. Me with (l. to r.) Sarah, Cortlandt, Thomas, Kristen

Retirement Party for me at our house in Bound Brook, June, 2001
Family, friends and Wagner College associates

Passau, Germany on Danube Cruise with Deipnos, 2004

Mike's 50th college reunion at Princeton, 2004

Our 50th Wedding Anniversary

Back row: Malcolm, Mary, Braden, Julie; Middle row: Cortlandt, Thomas, Kristen, Sarah; Front row: Brad, Lucas, Nicole, Mike, Me, Victoria, Carrie.

Printed in the United States
25626LVS00004BA/2

met Tory's to hold her transfixed. For several seconds their gazes locked and Tory felt as if Trask could see into her soul. Her throat tightened and her breath seemed trapped in her lungs.

"Senator McFadden," the D.A. was saying. "Would you describe in your own words why you came back to Sinclair and what you discovered?"

Trask tore his gaze away from Tory's and his voice was without inflection as he told the court about the series of events that had started with the anonymous letter he had received in Washington and had finally led to the arrest of Keith Wilson, as part of the Quarter Horse swindle that Trask's brother, Jason, was investigating when he was killed five years earlier.

Reporters were busy scribbling notes or drawing likenesses of the participants in the trial. The room was filled with faces of curious townspeople, many of whom Tory recognized. Anna Hutton sat with Tory, silently offering her support to her friend. Neva sat across the courtroom, her face white with strain. Several of the ranch hands were in the room, including Rex, who had already given his testimony. At Rex's side was his young wife, Belinda.

As Trask told his story, Tory sat transfixed. Though it was stifling hot in the old courtroom with the high ceilings, Tory shuddered and experienced the icy cold sensation of *deja vu*. Trask's shoulders slumped slightly and the smile and self-assurance that had always been with him had vanished.

This has been hard on him, Tory thought, realizing for the first time since Keith had confessed that Trask did care what happened to her. He was a man driven by principle and was forced to stalk anyone involved in the murder of his brother. And if the situation were reversed, and Keith had been the man murdered, wouldn't